Reviewers said this about
Night Shadows

A Detective Louis Martelli, NYPD, Mystery/Thriller

"The case in **Night Shadows** *develops with structural underpinnings and plot machinations so advanced even the most savvy of mystery readers will 'raise an eyebrow' to the skill used by Cohen."*
Gary Sorkin for *Pacific Book Review*

"In **Night Shadows,** *Cohen skillfully combines a unique creative imagination with a keen sense of investigative reporting, knowledge of police procedures, and an intuitive understanding of human nature...to draw the reader into the story."*
Richard Blake for *Reader Views*

"I cannot remember a time in the past decade when I picked up a mystery/thriller and was so surprised."
Russell D. James for *Hollywood Book Review*

"As a lawyer, it's always been disconcerting how Cohen sets himself up as judge, jury, and executioner, but I know his readers absolutely relish the idea."
Kerry Donahue, Esq.

"This novel, ripped from the headlines, should serve as a wakeup call to what increasingly appears to be an epidemic of child abuse, teenage rape, and teen suicide."
Susan Violante, Author of *Innocent War: Behind An Immigrant's Past*
italianaustinite.com, blogtalkradio.com/vioradio

For more information, visit:
www.theodore-cohen-novels.com
or your preferred on-line retailer

Other Novels
by
Theodore Jerome Cohen

*Death by Wall Street**
*House of Cards**
*Lilith**
Frozen in Time†
Unfinished Business†
End Game†
Cold Blood††
Full Circle

* A Detective Louis Martelli, NYPD, Mystery/Thriller
†The Antarctic Murders Trilogy
††The Antarctic Murders Trilogy, Books I, II, III in one Kindle
eBook edition

Visit us on the World Wide Web
http://www.theodore-cohen-novels.com

Night Shadows

Theodore Jerome Cohen

TJC Press

TJC Press
122 Shady Brook Drive
Langhorne, PA 19047-8027 USA
www.theodore-cohen-novels.com

First published 3/20/2014

ISBN-10: 0984920986 (sc)
ISBN-13: 978-0-9849209-8-3 (sc)
ISBN-10: 0984920935 (e)
ISBN-13: 978-0-9849209-3-8 (e)

Published in the United States of America

Cover photograph: Big Stock Photo
Front cover design by the author

Photo Credits:
Photograph of author: Susan Cohen, 2006

The views expressed in this work are solely those of the author.

Printed by CreateSpace, An Amazon.com Company
Available from Amazon.com, CreateSpace.com, and other retail outlets

Available on Kindle
eBook created by eBookConversion.com

Copyrights
and
Other Notes and Notices

A 'black and white' is a police patrol car.

Acela Express® is a registered trademark of the National Railroad Passenger Corporation

The Blue Screen of Death is displayed when a personal computer encounters an error from which it cannot recover. This is usually caused by an illegal operation being performed.

A 'bus' in police parlance is an ambulance.

Coke® is a registered trademark of Coca-Cola Company.

Corvette® automobiles are a product of the Chevrolet Division, General Motors LLC

Dirty Harry is a 1971 American crime thriller film produced and directed by Don Siegel, the first in the *Dirty Harry* series. Clint Eastwood played the title role. He carried a Smith & Wesson Model 29 revolver.

Facebook® is a registered trademark of Facebook, Inc.

Ford® automobiles, including the *Crown Victoria*®, are products of the Ford Motor Company

JPEG; Joint Photographic Experts Group; also jpg; format for photo images

Lamborghini® automobiles, including the *Huracán*®, are products of the Automobili Lamborghini S.p.A.

Police Unity Tour® is a registered trademark of Police Unity Tour, Inc.

Popsicle® is a registered trademark of Unilever, Inc.

Smith & Wesson® is a registered trademark of Smith & Wesson Holding Corp.

Stryker® is a registered trademark of Stryker Corporation

The New York Times® is a publication of The New York Times Company.

Dr. T. Theodore Fujita of the University of Chicago devised a six-category scale to classify U.S. tornadoes into six intensity categories, named F0-F5.

Twitter® is a registered trademark of Twitter, Inc.

WhitePages® is a registered trademark of WhitePages, Inc.

Who Are You, the theme song from the television show <u>CSI</u>, was composed by Pete Townsend and is the title track on The Who's 1978 release, *Who Are You.*

Abbreviations

1PP	One Police Plaza (NYPD Headquarters)
AM	Ante Meridiem; Before Midday
BC	Before Christ
CD	Compact Disc
CSU	Crime Scene Unit
DA	District Attorney
DC	District of Columbia
DOJ	Department of Justice
DNA	Deoxyribonucleic acid
EPUB	Electronic Publication (open standard for eBooks)
ER	Emergency Room
FBI	Federal Bureau of Investigation
HVAC	Heating, Ventilation, and Air Conditioning
I-81 N	Interstate (Highway) 81 North
IT	Information Technology
LA	Louisiana
LLC	Limited Liability Corporation
MBA	Master of Business Administration
MD	Doctor of Medicine
ME	Medical Examiner
MTA	Metropolitan Transportation Authority
N	North
NGI	Next Generation Identification (System; FBI)
NJ	New Jersey
NSOPW	National Sex Offender Public Website (US Department of Justice)
NY	New York
NYPD	New York Police Department
PDF	Proprietary Document Format (controlled by Adobe, Inc.)
PHD	Doctor of Philosophy,
PM	Post Meridiem; After Midday
STD	Sexuality Transmitted Disease
TV	Television (Receiver)
US	United States
VA	Veterans Affairs (formally, the US Department of Veterans Affairs)

Acronyms

ASAP	As Soon As Possible
SOL	Shit Out of Luck
WITSEC	WITness SECurity (Program)

Codes

10-4	Police Ten Code ('acknowledge')
10-20 or '20'	Police Ten Code ('location')

To those for whom there was no justice

■

Dearly beloved, avenge not yourselves, but rather give place unto wrath: for it is written, Vengeance is mine; I will repay, saith the Lord.

Romans 12:19
King James Version

What most people don't seem to understand is that sometimes, He subcontracts the work!

Detective-Investigator Louis Martelli
NYPD

■

Foreword

For a modern society, the statistics on child sexual abuse in the United States not only are staggering but also abhorrent. According to the US Department of Justice's National Sex Offender Public Website (NSOPW),[1] 33% of sexual assaults occur when the victim is between the ages of 12 and 17. Importantly, 82% of all juvenile victims of sexual abuse are female, with about one in five female high school students reporting physical and/or sexual abuse by a dating partner. Even more distressing is the fact that teens 16 to 19 years of age were three-and-one-half times more likely than the general population to be victims of rape, attempted rape, or sexual assault.

Anyone who has followed the day-to-day news in the US and Canada should not be surprised by these statistics. The media has put real names to the numbers . . . names such as Daisy Colemen of Maryville, Missouri, who, after accusing a high school senior of sexual assault and was bullied, was hospitalized after a suicide attempt. Or Rehtaeh Parsons from Halifax, Nova Scotia, who after allegedly being gang-raped and bullied, was hospitalized after she tried to hang herself on April 4, 2013. She was taken off life support three days later. Colman and Parsons were not alone. According to Suicide.org, numerous rape victims have suicidal thoughts; many die by suicide.[2]

Nor do the living escape their tormenters. With 90% of teens and young adults online, the potential for abuse is significant, especially with the greater majority of those having a profile

---

[1] http://www.nsopr.gov/en/Education/FactsMythsStatistics?AspxAutoDetectCookieSupport=1 [See this reference for additional references to the statistics cited.]
[2] http://www.suicide.org/rape-victims-prone-to-suicide.html

on a social network. In fact, nearly 80% of teens send and receive photos and videos online, some almost certainly pornographic. Nude selfies are not uncommon, with revenge porn—defined as sexually explicit media that are publicly shared online without the consent of the pictured individual[3]—becoming increasingly common. The Internet always was a dangerous neighborhood; with time it has become more so, and more toxic, as well.

I don't know if child sexual abuse has yet reached what the US and other health authorities might consider 'epidemic proportions.' But I do know I am seeing an increasing number of cases in the newspaper, on television, and on the Internet, among other media, where young women are assaulted and raped, are subsequently harassed, and bullied by their attackers and/or peers, and in some cases, are driven to suicide. And the pity of it is, for many of these victims, there is no justice.

This novel is an attempt to shine a spotlight on the problem of teen rape. Though many may see it as another Detective Louis Martelli, NYPD 'ripped from the headlines' mystery/thriller, know it is fiction through and through . . . the characters, the crimes, the dialogue, *everything*. It's a fabrication. But still, this is an important story if for no other reason than to raise awareness of a scourge that is harming our children, the most precious part of our lives.

Theodore Jerome Cohen
March 1, 2014

---

[3] http://en.wikipedia.org/wiki/Revenge_porn

Acknowledgements

I would be lost without my wife Susan, who provided vital suggestions, insightful editing, and most importantly, unswerving support during the development of the manuscript. She is the love of my life, my soulmate, and my 'partner in crime.' I gratefully acknowledge a suggestion from Sandra Prime that inspired me to add a vital subplot to the storyline. Bob Mehta of eBookConversion.com provided many useful suggestions regarding the production of the Kindle version as well as guidance pertaining to the distribution of the book. Stephanie Rubin and Dr. Martin Halpern generously gave of their time to root out those mischievous typos and other errors that somehow eluded me in draft after draft.

One

D eputy Coroner Michael Antonetti had just finished making a deep Y-shaped incision in Trent Morrison's chest—shoulder-to-shoulder meeting at the breast bone and extending down to the pubic bone—and was about to peel back the skin, muscle, and soft tissue using a scalpel when he heard the distinctive footsteps of NYPD Detective-Investigator Louis Martelli behind him. "Ah, Louis, how good of you to come so quickly. I think you'll find this interesting!"

Antonetti never looked up as he pulled the chest flap over Morrison's face. With the ribcage and neck muscles exposed, he cut the sides of the man's ribcage.

Martelli, now standing to the left of his old friend, nodded *Hello* to Antonetti's assistant, Latonya Williams. "Well, you said it was important, Michael."

Antonetti, focused on removing the soft tissue behind the chest plate, muttered something unintelligible, which Martelli took either as affirmation of the situation's importance or a mild expletive.

While waiting for the coroner to finish preparing the chest cavity for organ extraction, Martelli grabbed the manila folder at the head of the cadaver dissection table and began reviewing Morrison's file. "Hey, this is the guy they found in Tribeca yesterday morning. I read about it in the *Times*. He overdosed on heroin and alcohol. No wonder I smelled booze when I got close to the body."

"One and the same, Louis. Meet Mr. Trent Morrison, commodity futures trader, in his mid-30s, single, living the high life . . . perhaps a little *too* high. His housekeeper found him when she came to work around 8 AM. The guy was still sitting on the couch in his living room on the third floor with music playing on the stereo and a half-empty glass of wine on the coffee table."

Antonetti reached into Morrison's chest cavity. After opening the pulmonary artery to search for a blood clot, he systematically removed first the heart, which he handed to Williams for weighing, and then the lungs, first the left, and then the right, which she also weighed. After weighing, Williams set each organ aside in its own stainless steel bowl. When she and Dr. Antonetti were finished at the autopsy table, she would prepare tissue samples of the organs for shipment to the pathologist.

Martelli shrugged. "So, the guy overdosed. I see it all the time. Rich, poor, makes no difference. Drugs are an equal-opportunity killer. This case looks open and shut. From what I read in the newspaper this morning, the housekeeper said the door to the townhouse was locked when she arrived, and there were no signs of forced entry. What's the problem?"

"Everything you said is correct, Louis. I can tell you as well there appeared to be no signs a third party was in the apartment with him when he died. I was at the townhouse yesterday morning with the black and white that responded to the call. Everything points to the man having been alone when he overdosed, but—"

Martelli raised his eyebrows. "Uh-oh, I don't like the sound of this—"

"But some things don't add up."

"Such as—"

"The needle was found stuck in his right arm. Yet Morrison is right-handed. He wore his watch on his left wrist. I would have expected him to have used his right hand to inject himself in his *left* arm.

"And something else I found strange, Louis."

"What's that?"

"He wasn't a user. At least he currently wasn't mainlining heroin. There are no other fresh needle marks on either arm. I also found it interesting—" Antonetti stopped talking momentarily while he placed Morrison's liver in Williams's hands. He continued. "I found it interesting his arm wasn't tied off where I'd expect it to be."

"What do you mean?"

"Well, the needle was found in his upper forearm. In that case, the arm should have been tied off just above the elbow. But the tourniquet on Morrison's arm was found below his elbow."

Martelli examined Morrison's right arm. The tie-off and injection sites were still clearly visible. "Maybe he was too drunk to know what he was doing."

"I doubt it. From what I read in the newspapers, Morrison was a former addict. Records—and God knows how the newspapers got a hold of them—show he was found using drugs as a teenager and spent two months in rehab. He started using again some years ago and spent four months in a drug treatment center in Albany in 2010. I found traces of old needle marks on his body, mostly on his left arm and left leg. None was fresh. Frankly, I don't think he had been 'using' since he was released from rehab in Albany.

"If you want my opinion, the man consumed a large quantity of alcohol sometime late yesterday and someone injected heroin into his system *after* he passed out. The alcohol exacerbated the heroin's effect on his central nervous system, slowing the functions that regulated his heart rate and breathing. He died almost instantly after he was injected."

"About what time did you place his death?"

"From his body temperature, ten PM, give or take an hour."

Martelli stroked his chin. "So, you're saying this is a homicide."

"I'm saying his death is suspicious. I'm certainly not ready to rule out the possibility it was accidental and most likely the result of a drug overdose. But we need to know considerably more about the events leading up to his death and the discovery of his body before I'll be ready to sign his death certificate."

Antonetti proceeded to cut Morrison's kidneys from his chest cavity. He handed them to Williams for weighing and the preparation of tissue samples for the pathologist. Next he removed the man's stomach and intestines, which he spent little time examining, given his knowledge about the cause and time of death. Williams also took these organs for weighing and subsequent dissection.

With work on the body cavity completed, Antonetti and Williams turned their attention to the victim's head. Donning a face shield, and after asking Martelli to step back, the coroner deftly used a Stryker saw to open the man's skull, facilitating the extraction of the brain. Antonetti then severed the brain's connection to the cranial nerves and spinal cord before lifting the organ from the skull and handing it to Williams. She, in turn, placed it in a large container of formalin for preservation.

Martelli watched intently. He was continually fascinated by how Antonetti and his colleagues were able to determine what they did from the remains of the deceased and other evidence found on the body, even after days or weeks if not years had passed between the time of death and the performance of the autopsy.

"I think we're just about finished here for the time being," announced Antonetti. "We still have a ton of work to do on the dissection table, but we'll get to that in short order.

"Latonya, would you please close the body while I talk with Louis?"

The two men walked to Antonetti's cluttered desk and sat. Antonetti was about to speak when Williams called out. "I think you better see this, Dr. Antonetti." She held up a round, tarnished object in her gloved right hand. It was a coin.

Two

'W hat the hell is that?" exclaimed Antonetti as he and Martelli jumped up and raced back to the autopsy table.

"I was working on the head and when I chanced to turn it to the left," explained Williams, "I must have dislodged it from under his tongue." She placed the coin in a plastic evidence bag and handed it to Antonetti.

The coroner held it up to the light. "Well, I'll be damned, Louis . . . a Charon's obol. It appears to be made of bronze."

"A *what?*" Martelli asked.

"It's a coin from the old Greek and Latin literature. It was used as payment for Charon, the ferryman who took souls across the river dividing the world of the living from the world of the dead. The ancient Greeks and Romans were primarily associated with this custom, but you also find it used in the ancient Western European cultures, even into the early 20th century."

"Well, it's pretty clear someone is playing with us, Michael, and more to the point, at the least, it indicates someone was with Morrison when he died, if not helping him into the next world."

Martelli reached into his pocket, drew out his cell phone, and with a swipe of the screen and a few keystrokes, was connected with his partner, Detective-Specialist Sean O'Keeffe.

"What's up, Lou?"

"Sean, that Morrison guy, the one they thought overdosed in Tribeca the other night . . . there's a good possibility we may be dealing with a homicide. Get ahold of Morrison's housekeeper and have her open the place for us in an hour. We need to toss it. I'll explain everything when I get there."

"Gotcha covered, man."

Martelli ended the call and placing the phone in his jacket pocket, headed for the door as fast as his new prosthetic leg would allow.

Martelli had been the crew member aboard a Black Hawk helicopter that was shot down in the April, 2003 invasion of Baghdad during Operation Iraqi Freedom. Now, with the help of a prosthetic leg, he walked with a slight limp. He worked for NYPD under a special waiver issued by the mayor. 'Hey,' he always reminded those who asked about his injury, 'at least I'm alive. That's more than I can say for the pilot and copilot, who never made it out of the chopper!'

After Martelli returned home from Walter Reed National Military Medical Center following his release from the Army, he was plagued by nightmares. Night after night Stephanie, his wife, was awakened by his screams . . . screams of a desperate man yelling to the pilot and copilot of their ill-fated Black Hawk, urging them to free themselves from the debris in the cockpit and fight their way back through the flames to the rear sliding door, where he stood waiting for them. She knew when he saw they could not get out of the cockpit, despite his having a shattered left leg and second-degree burns on his hip, that he had fought his way to the front of the aircraft, only to be driven back by the intense heat from fuel that had ignited. His last memory before he blacked out was of the cries from the cockpit . . . desperate cries for help that he never was able to answer . . . desperate cries that he heard, over and over again in his nightmares, until he thought he would go insane.

It was Stephanie who was always there when that happened, soothing him, changing the bed sheets that had become drenched in sweat, and assuring him that 'this, too, shall pass' and tomorrow would be a better day.

Following an incident in which an FBI agent accidentally fired a slug into his prosthesis during the take-down of a gang of cigarette smugglers, and after a murderer he was chasing stuck a syringe into the same device, Martelli applied to the VA for a new prosthesis. It took him more than two months to obtain a replacement. At first, the US Department of Veterans Affairs insisted the old one could be repaired. When Martelli protested, the government asserted budgetary restrictions prevented them from providing him with a new device. Finally, Stephanie went to their congressman's office and asked that the representative intervene on Martelli's behalf. Martelli was fitted for a new prosthesis two weeks later.

That said, Martelli insists to this day it was his visit to the VA—during which he told an administrator the VA had two weeks to schedule a fitting or he would come back and stick his old leg where the Sun didn't shine—that changed the government's mind. Those who knew him never doubted his version of the story. Martelli always joked, euphemistically, that you could go far in this world with a gun and a smile, and sometimes, you didn't even need to smile.

"How's the new leg, Louis?" Antonetti shouted as Martelli disappeared through the morgue's double doors.

"Couldn't be better, Michael!" Martelli shouted back. "I'll have it whipped into shape in no time!"

Three

It was shortly before 11 AM when Martelli pulled his *Crown Vic* to the curb in front of Morrison's Tribeca townhouse. He could see Sean's sedan already parked on the other side of the street.

The neighborhood was developed in the late 18th century, and today, is one of the tonier areas of New York City. With the area's industrial base erased by the 1960s, a major change ensued that, beginning in the 1980s, saw Tribeca transformed into an upscale residential area. Today, homes and condominiums south of Canal Street between Broadway and West Street, extending south to Chambers Street, sell well into the millions, and Morrison's easily was worth something north of $10 million.

The housekeeper, Maria Cordero, met Martelli outside, at the front door. The building now was considered a crime scene, so she had been ordered not to enter the townhouse without a police escort until the NYPD released it to Mr. Morrison's estate.

"Thanks for meeting us, *Señora Cordero*. I will have to ask you for the keys to the townhouse, now that we're looking into things a bit more. I'm sure you understand."

"Oh, yes . . . *si* . . . I understand, *Señor. ¡Qué horror!* So *horrible* what happened to *Señor Morrison.* He was always so good to me. I was with him five years. He always treated me so good. He always gave me a generous gift at Christmas—"

The woman turned away from Martelli, and taking a handkerchief from her purse, began dabbing her eyes.

Martelli gave her a moment to compose herself. "Did you notice anything different about him in the last few days before his death, *Señora?*"

"Oh, no, he was always very cheerful . . . very *simpatico.* I saw him that morning when he was leaving. He waved and said for me to have wonderful day. It was like he didn't have a care in the world."

"Can you think of anyone who would have wanted to harm him, perhaps someone he had argued with on the telephone in the days preceding his death?"

Cordero was taken aback by Martelli's question. "Oh my. I certainly did not listen to his calls. Besides, *Señor,* I never heard his *teléfono* ring. He always used *un teléfono móvil.*"

"On last thing, *Señora Cordero.* On what floor is Mr. Morrison's bedroom?"

"The top floor, *Señor.*"

"*Muchas gracious, Señora.* If we have any further questions, we'll be in contact. Meantime, here is a receipt from the NYPD for the keys to the townhouse. Please be sure to keep it in a safe place should you ever need to show it to someone."

The housekeeper turned the keys over to Martelli. Putting the receipt in her purse, she made her way down the street toward the bus stop.

Martelli took the townhouse's elevator to the top floor. O'Keeffe was already there, going through papers and other artifacts in the master suite. The townhouse had four bedrooms and as many baths, one for each bedroom. According to information provided to police by the housekeeper, the entire house had recently been renovated, and comprised something on the order of 4,000 square feet . . . at least she heard her boss speak of that number when talking on the phone to his contractor. In addition to a large expanse of landscaped space in the rear, the unit also included a fenced-in roof deck.

The master suite on the 4th level featured soaring windows and 18-foot loft-like ceilings. A curved, Statuario white marble grand staircase with a white Italian marble banister trimmed with gold leaf connected the master suite to the floor beneath, which housed the living and dining rooms used for entertaining. The remaining three bedrooms were on the second while the first floor housed the kitchen and pantry. As well, the lower level provided garage space for Morrison's bright yellow Lamborghini.

"Not bad," O'Keeffe deadpanned, "Susan and I could get used to this once we're married." O'Keeffe and Dr. Susan Allerton of Lake George, NY, were engaged, something that provided Martelli with no end of opportunities to joke with his partner regarding wedded bliss. On one occasion, when Sean mentioned his days as a bachelor might be numbered, Martelli gleefully recommended he see a priest as soon as possible to receive his last rites.

"Find anything, Sean?"

"Yeah, the guy is a graduate of the Louis Martelli School of Office Management!"

The floor in Martelli's office is covered with piles of documents from closed and open cases, some going back ten years or more. Martelli knows where every document is. Cleaning up his office would merely confuse him for the next six months. Hence, what appears to visitors as one of the most cluttered offices in the precinct actually constitutes what Martelli proudly proclaims as 'my whole-office, readily expandable, easily accessible, open-source filing system.'

The same could be said of Morrison's home office. Located in a wood-paneled room adjacent to his sleeping quarters that offered a magnificent view of the surrounding area, the floors were covered with stacks of books, reports, newspapers, magazines, and various documents, almost all of which were related to his work as a commodity futures trader with Bernstein, Fallen & Mark, LLC, one of the most prestigious firms in the industry.

"Just the usual," continued O'Keeffe, "laptop computer, two cell phones—one may be his private phone, the other a company-provided device—lots of financial reports, some personal correspondence, check books, and so forth. I've bagged and tagged what I thought might be relevant. I also found his calendar, telephone log, credit card receipts, lots of yellow stickies—the guy was a freak when it came to using those things . . . they're all over the place—and a few other things we can go over back at the precinct once we log it into the Evidence Room at 1PP."

"Great! I'll help you get the evidence to your car. I'm very anxious for Dugan to get her hands on that computer and the two cell phones. They may be the best sources of leads we have at this point in addition to his correspondence and the various notes you've grabbed."

■ *Theodore Jerome Cohen*

Four

"Waddaya got for me, Missy?" It was a little after 7 AM the next morning when Martelli walked into Principal Information Technology Specialist Missy Dugan's laboratory in the basement of 1PP. Dugan began programming microprocessors—in binary, no less—in the mid-1970s when her dad brought home a Texas Instruments demonstration kit programmable by means of eight toggle switches. By late 1980, at age 12, she was into hacking, breaking the security features used to protect games hidden on the outer sectors of floppy disks. Give her an electronic device, *any device,* and within 60 seconds she could make it work, regardless of whether or not the instruction manual was available. And when it came to software, she could run rings around most of the whiz kids employed by today's social networking corporations. It was only her dedication to the NYPD in general and Martelli in particular that kept her in the Department's service.

"Scheesch, you are the impatient one, aren't you?!"

"Well, I figured you had a few hours to go through his computer and cell phones, so obviously, you must have solved the case for me by now."

"Martelli, you are so full of it. I don't know how Stephanie and the kids even put up with you. But yes, in between all the other things I have to do for the 40,000 members of New York's Finest, I did take a few seconds to look at your evidence in the Morrison case."

"So?"

"So, for one thing, your Mr. Morrison had reservations for two at the Corinthian, a pretty swank restaurant in the East Village, at 8 PM on the night of his demise. He placed the reservation using his personal cell phone the night before his death. Here's the number." She handed Martelli a piece of paper on which was written the restaurant's telephone number.

"This could be a significant lead, Missy. Whoever had dinner with Morrison probably was the last person to see him alive!"

"Well, don't get your hopes up, Martelli."

"Waddaya talking about? This could break the case!"

"Calm down, Lou. I went back to the Evidence Room and pulled all the credit card receipts I could find. I found one time-stamped at 9:24 PM from the Corinthian for $81.98. Now, even a glance online at the Corinthian's menu will tell you a bill like that would barely cover a few drinks and a shrimp cocktail. Dinner for two should have run well beyond $300, not including drinks.

"My guess is, whoever he was supposed to meet stood him up. But perhaps someone at the restaurant can fill in the blanks."

"And that's it? With everything in the evidence box, *that's it*? Come on, Missy. You're my 'go-to' gal, the one who works miracles. Time to pull a rabbit out of your hat!"

"Give me a break! But now that you ask, here's one for you. If you look at his business cell phone and specifically at the call he received *just* before he called for reservations at the Corinthian, you'll see it came from a payphone."

"A payphone? Do they even have those anymore?"

"In a few places around the city. This one is at the Port Authority Bus Terminal on 8th Avenue. My guess is, whoever he was meeting for dinner came into town by bus and called him from a payphone."

"That makes no sense. Almost anyone who travels today carries a cell phone. Why use a payphone?"

"Well duh! So the call couldn't be traced to a specific person."

Martelli smiled. "Ah, yes, but there are cameras all over the bus station, and some are most certainly are focused on payphones."

"True, my liege, which is why I've already pulled down the video from all of the cameras in the bus terminal around the time of the call. Based on the payphone's telephone number, I was able to locate the phone. Here's the video of your caller."

Dugan turned to her computer. With a few keystrokes, her monitor came alive. As she and Martelli watched, a shadowy figure approached the payphone from the right, being careful to hide his or her face from the camera. "Whoever it was, Lou, they certainly were aware of where the cameras were located."

"Dammit, Missy, it's like watching a shadow in the dark of night. I can't even tell if it's a man or a woman."

"My bets are on it being a woman . . . unless the guy's carrying a man-purse. You can barely see the outline of a shoulder strap and the purse under her arm." She pointed the strap out to him on the screen.

Martelli looked disheartened. "Well, that eliminates half the population."

Dugan ignored his sarcasm. "And, for your edification and enjoyment, know that five busses arrived within 15 minutes of the call being made to Morrison. They came from Boston, Detroit, Philadelphia, Washington, DC, and Syracuse. Of course, several of the women aboard those busses had substantial purses with over-the-shoulder straps."

"So, we're pretty well fucked when it comes to knowing which bus our person of interest used to get to New York, right?"

"Oh, ye of little faith! When I was a little girl, my father used to make us laugh by running our 8mm home movies backwards. Instead of watching kids jump out from behind a snow drift, we watched as everyone jumped up and disappeared behind the snow.

"I did the same thing here, running the video from the surveillance cameras in reverse. I never got a good look at the woman's face—she was careful to keep it shielded from the cameras—but there's no question she came in on the bus from Syracuse . . . or maybe the one from Washington, DC."

"What do you mean 'Syracuse . . . *or Washington, DC*?' Which one is it?"

"Well, shit, I don't know. The end of the concourse was poorly lit, and the busses from Syracuse and DC pulled in one right after the other. I looked at the video three times and still couldn't make out which bus that woman stepped from."

Martelli took a big breath and let it out slowly. "Okay, I understand. If you had to choose, which one would it be?"

Missy thought for a minute. "I'd say your person of interest came in from upstate, Lou."

"That's terrific, Missy. Keep working the evidence and let me know what you find. In the meantime, Sean and I will hit the Corinthian and see if anyone remembers seeing Morrison or his guest."

"Will do, Lou. By the way, what's with the Charon's obol in the vic's mouth?"

Her question took Martelli by surprise. "How did you find out about that?"

She laughed. "Haven't you learned by now? I know everything that goes on inside 1PP.

"That bronze coin you found in the vic's mouth is from the Black Sea region. The last time I heard about one of those was in high school, in Mrs. Wilson's ancient history class."

Five

It was mid-afternoon when Martelli and O'Keeffe pulled up in front of the Corinthian and made their way to the bar.

"What'll it be, gents?" asked the bartender as he placed two cocktail napkins in front of them.

Martelli and O'Keeffe flashed their badges. "Sorry, we're on duty. Official police business, I'm afraid," said Martelli.

O'Keeffe pulled a picture of Morrison from his suit jacket and showed it to the bartender. "Do you recognize this man?"

"Yes, of course, that's Mr. Morrison. He was a regular here. Terrible what happened. I can't imagine him doing this to himself. I saw him earlier that evening. He was in great spirits, said he was meeting an old friend for dinner, kept looking at his watch and over toward the door, and finally was shown to his table around 8 PM or so.

"Oh, here's the matre'd. Perhaps he can tell you more. Joseph, Joseph! These men are from the Police Department. They're asking about Mr. Morrison."

The matre'd walked to the bar. "I'm Joseph Archer. May I be of service, gentleman?"

23

O'Keeffe showed him the picture of Morrison. "Oh, yes. Mr. Morrison. What a tragedy. Terrible, simply terrible. He was in here just the other night . . . very excited about having dinner with an old friend who he said had come to town the night before. Unfortunately, the party apparently was unable to make it for one reason or another."

"Do you know if Mr. Morrison received any calls from this person, explaining, perhaps, why she could not meet him?"

"No, I distinctly remember him saying how surprised he was that he didn't hear from her. And he also was surprised he could not reach her at the number she had used to contact him. He said the phone just rang and rang, but no one answered."

Martelli looked at O'Keeffe. They understood. Few people, if any, would pick up a ringing payphone in a metropolitan bus terminal.

O'Keeffe continued. "What did he do then?"

"He had a few drinks and a small appetizer, tried his party's phone a few more times, waited an hour or so—maybe an hour and a half—paid his bill, and departed. I think he must have taken a cab because he didn't ask me to validate a parking ticket. That was the last time I saw him."

Martelli looked around the restaurant. "I see you have an extensive array of surveillance cameras. Do you have cameras outside as well?"

"We maintain two cameras outside. One is in the back covering the rear entrance and trash bin, and one is in the front, though the view there is partially obscured by the canopy over the walkway to the front door."

"Would it be possible to have a CD containing the video from the camera over the front door for the evening Mr. Morrison was here . . . say, from an hour before he arrived to an hour after he left?"

The matre'd nodded. "Of course. I'll have our IT person prepare a copy as soon as he gets in around 4 PM or so. Where shall I send it?"

Martelli gave him his card. "Please have it couriered to me, if you would. It would be immensely helpful."

"Consider it done, gentlemen."

■ Theodore Jerome Cohen

<u>Six</u>

'**L**ou, I thought you'd never get here. I was about to leave for dinner, but didn't want to miss you. Do you have the CD from the restaurant?" Dugan could barely contain her excitement.

"Right here." He handed her the CD from the surveillance camera over the front entrance at the Corinthian. In an instant, her monitor came alive with the recorded images from the night Morrison last visited the restaurant.

"Fast forward to around 9:15 PM, or so, Missy, and watch for a cab to pull up."

Dugan advanced the CD as they watched both the action on her monitor and the date-time stamp in the upper left-hand corner of the screen. Suddenly Martelli almost jumped out of his shoes.

"Freeze the action!"

Dugan paused the CD. They both stared at a shadowy figure of a woman they had seen walk to the entrance but stay to one side of the canopy. Smartly dressed in a trim, black, well-tailored suit, she wore a broad-brimmed hat with a dark veil

27

to conceal her face. She stood there, holding her clutch purse in front of her, as if waiting for a cab.

"Okay, Missy, start the CD rolling again, but keep it moving slowly."

As the video played, the doorman was seen approaching the woman twice, apparently to inquire if she needed a cab. Both times she waved him off. Minutes passed, and the clock on the screen now read 9:27 PM. A man was seen leaving the restaurant. The woman moved quickly to intercept him as he signaled the doorman for a cab. The man and woman greeted each other like old friends, and with a cab now at the curb and the doorman tipped, the couple was driven off into the night.

"There goes Morrison with our mystery woman, Missy. I'll bet a year's salary she's our murderer! Did you get the cab's license number?"

"Sure did. Hold on. I'll get you the cabby's company and registration." It took her less than a minute to comb through the databases of the city's Taxi and Limousine Division. Grabbing a piece of paper, she wrote down the address of the cab company and the name of the driver. "Perhaps this guy can tell you something."

Seven

Kofi Agyeman had been driving cab in New York City since arriving in this country from Ghana almost ten years earlier. He was one of more than 40 drivers who worked for the New York All-Boro Taxi Corporation, and according to the owner, was one of the more dependable.

"Kofi? Sure, he's one of our best," boasted Sol Kaplan, the company's manager. "Let me see where he is."

Kaplan picked up his cell phone, dialed a number, and within seconds was talking to Agyeman. "What's your '20?'"

Kaplan nodded as he listened to his driver. "Okay. Hang on."

Kaplan turned to Martelli. "He's just about to drop a fare a mile or so from here. Should I have him come back to the shop?"

Martelli nodded. "That would make it easy all around."

"Kofi, come back to the shop as soon as you drop your fare. I need to see you about something. It won't take long."
Kaplan nodded, indicating, apparently, Agyeman would comply. "Okay, see you in a few minutes."

It was about ten minutes before Agyeman pulled his cab into the garage, stepped out, and walked over to where Kaplan, Martelli, and O'Keeffe were waiting.

"Kofi, these men are detectives from the New York Police Department." Martelli and O'Keeffe flashed their badges.

Agyeman's eyes grew as big as silver dollars. Kaplan started to laugh, putting his hands up, palms out, in front of him. "Don't worry, don't worry . . . you've done nothing wrong. In fact, they think you may be able to help them."

Agyeman breathed a sigh of relief, and even managed a faint smile. "How can I help you, sirs?" It was clear that even after ten years, he still struggled with the English language.

O'Keeffe took the picture of Morrison out of his suit jacket and showed it to Agyeman. "We believe you picked up this man at the Corinthian the night before last. Can you confirm that?"

"Oh, yes, I remember him. He was in very good mood and gave me big tip."

"We know he was with a woman. Did you happen to see her face or hear any of their discussion? Anything you can tell us about her would be most helpful."

"I remember her, too. Sadly, I did not see her face. It was covered in black veil." Agyeman drew his hands across his eyes, making the sign of a veil.

"They talk and talk about old times and how many years have passed since they saw each other."

"Did he call her by name," asked O'Keeffe.

"No, he never say her name."

O'Keeffe pressed on. "Mr. Agyeman, can you remember anything else about them or what they said, anything at all?"

"I am so sorry, but traffic was heavy. I couldn't pay attention to them. Please understand."

"Can you tell us what time you dropped them off, and where?" asked Martelli.

"Oh, yes. Please . . . one minute." He held up his forefinger.

Agyeman turned and walked briskly to his cab, returning with his taxi trip log. Paging through the booklet, he came to the sought-after information. "I drop them in Tribeca—perhaps at gentleman's residence—at 9:48 PM. Then, I stay parked in front of house for a few minutes to complete my log."

Martelli nodded. "What did you see then?"

"The gentleman opened the door and they went in. That's all I remember."
Martelli nodded. "Thank you, Mr. Agyeman, you've been most helpful.

"Mr. Kaplan, we'll need a copy of that page of the log, if that's possible."

"Not a problem, Detective."

Eight

'**D**ammit, Tiffany, you blew the breaker again! Can't I even shave in peace without your goddam hair dryer taking down the entire East Coast power grid?"

The second floor of the Martelli household once again had been plunged into darkness as the family was preparing for school and work. The time was 6:05 AM. Stephanie already was in the kitchen, preparing breakfast. Rob, their teenage son, had finished dressing and was on his way downstairs when the latest in their never-ending series of electrical catastrophes occurred.

"I'll reset the breaker, Dad. It'll just take a minute."

"Stephanie, I thought you said the electrician was going to replace the breaker yesterday."

"No, Lou," Stephanie shouted up the stairs, "he's coming late tomorrow afternoon. I'll have to take off work early to meet him, but what choice do we have? And by the way, you owe the Swearing Jar $10 for your outbursts this morning."

The Swearing Jar, which stood on the kitchen counter, held the money collected from family members for their 'speech infractions.' Affixed to it was a large sign: VEGAS OR BUST! Most of the money was contributed by Martelli, who was fined $5 per swear word. Stephanie and the children paid more modest fines, a mere $1 per foul word.

Not that Stephanie was a shy wallflower when it came to the language she used in voicing an opinion. She managed the heating, ventilation, and air conditioning shop where she worked with an iron fist. More than one sheet metal worker found himself bounced onto the street—"You know what you can do with your union!"—when he dared to show up late for a job or challenge her authority.

The annual trip to Las Vegas by the Family Martelli had a two-fold purpose: it gave Stephanie and the children a chance to get away from Brooklyn during Spring Break, and more importantly, at least to Martelli, it provided an opportunity for him to get together with his old war buddies and play some down and dirty poker.

Not that his family didn't see through Martelli and what was going on in those late-night poker games. The children may not have known the entire truth about their father's youth in general and his skills with cards in particular, but Stephanie did. With his father working odd hours as a police officer for the NYPD and his mother taking odd jobs to keep the family in groceries, Martelli, as a boy, had little in the way of supervision at home, day or night. It wasn't long before he was running numbers for local mobsters, hustling cards, working as a thimblerigger of a shell game on Broadway, picking pockets on the subway, and in general, heading for a life of crime, if not a long stay in one of New York State's prison complexes.

Given Martelli's behavior throughout his high school years, his father, immediately upon Louis's graduation from high school, drove his son to the Army recruiter's office and 'helped' him enlist. The Army was good to Martelli, and it was in Camp Udairi in Kuwait before the invasion of Iraq, among other places, where he honed his card-playing skills.

Of course, he sometimes took liberties with the card deck, as did those with whom he played. In a word, everyone knew everyone else cheated. After a while, the challenge became one of determining who could cheat the best. To this day, when Martelli got together with the men with whom he served in Kosovo, Kuwait, and Iraq, they *all* cheated. It was expected. In fact, the object of their time together in Las Vegas was not to win, but to see who could catch the other guys dealing from the bottom of the deck and otherwise manipulating the cards. And when all was said and done, every last dime on the table was contributed to the *Police Unity Tour* to help the families of law enforcement officers who died in the line of duty.

With the electricity on the second floor restored, it was not long before the family was seated at the kitchen table for breakfast. Tiffany was busy texting her boyfriend, Jeff Romano, to confirm when he would pick her up for school. This was the only exception made for the use of cell phones at the table. Violations of the house rule meant the loss of cell phone privileges for a day, something, according to Tiffany, that was akin to medieval torture.

"So, Rob, you're taking ancient history in high school, right?"

Rob looked up from his bowl of cereal with an inquisitive look on his face. "Ahhhh, yes," he said apprehensively, not knowing what to expect.

"I need your help. We have a case where a coin was found in the mouth of the victim."

Tiffany put her hand to her mouth. "Ewww, Daddy. Do you have to talk about it while were having breakfast?"

Rob was unfazed. "Seriously, Dad?"

"I'm being perfectly serious. What can you tell me about this practice?"

"Well, according to Mr. Sherman, my history teacher, in ancient times, people in some cultures placed a coin in the mouth of a dead person before burial. The Greek and Latin writings we studied specified the coin as an obol. It was meant as payment—perhaps a bribe—for Charon."

"Who's he?" Tiffany piped up.

Rob smiled. It wasn't often he got to expound on any subject in the presence of his know-it-all older sister. "He was the ferryman who took souls across the river separating the world of the living from the world of the dead."

The Martelli's son indeed had learned his ancient history well. The custom of placing a coin in the mouth of the deceased can be traced in Greek and Latin literature to the late fifth century BC. It was payment to the boatman for taking a soul across the River Styx into the underworld—also called Hades. Actually, the custom of placing coins in the mouth of the deceased at the time of death or burial is mentioned widely in the literature of many cultures. As well, there have been instances where multiple coins were placed in various locations on a body.

"Oh, now I remember," Tiffany chimed in, "Charon's obol. Yes, of course. Some people believe it also was used as a seal to protect the deceased's soul or to prevent the deceased's soul from returning. Every kid learns that in high school. Mr. Sherman even brought one to school. He said he bought it from a local coin dealer. It was cool."

Stephanie smiled, nodded, and gave her husband a smug look. "Well, haven't we raised a pair of geniuses, Lou?"

If Martelli heard her, he didn't respond.

"Lou, did you hear me?"

Martelli nodded his head, though he appeared to be off in another world by himself. Then, he suddenly returned to Earth. "Yes . . . yes . . . they *are* geniuses! And they just gave me an idea. Thanks, guys!"

He jumped from the table, and half walking, half skipping into the living room because of his prosthesis, grabbed his cell phone from his suit jacket and dialed O'Keeffe.

"Sean, Morrison was a commodity futures trader. He couldn't have gotten his license without having undergone a full security background check. Pull everything you can on him from the National Futures Association and any other sources you can find. I want to know where he grew up, where he went to school . . . *everything!* I think he knew his killer, perhaps well. In fact, I suspect they went to school together at some point."

"I'll get right on it, Lou."

"I'm on my way in. We can discuss what you find when I get there."

<u>Nine</u>

'I got what you wanted Lou. Morrison was born in 1978 to Richard and Mary Morrison, who lived on an estate just south of Jamesville, New York, near Syracuse. His old man was a stock broker and his mother was a stay-at-home mom who busied herself with charities and the like. Both are deceased—auto accident. He attended private schools throughout his youth, finally ending up in the area's prestigious co-ed Marquis de La Fayette High School. Here he excelled at both academics and sports. In fact, he was the captain of the school's football team in his junior and senior years."

"Sounds good, so far."

"Yes, but we also know from what had been printed in the local newspapers that the wheels came off the wagon sometime in his junior year when it was discovered he was using drugs. As a result, he entered a rehab facility for two months during the summer between his junior and senior years. This, of course, wouldn't show up in the National Futures Association's data, given he was a minor at the time."

"Okay, and then what?"

"He graduated and went on to earn a BS in Business and an MBA, both at well-known Eastern business schools, before joining Bernstein, Fallen & Mark. Apparently he's worked only for them since leaving school."

"My gut tells me this crime had its roots in something that happened back in Morrison's junior or senior year of high school. Still, finding that coin in his mouth is simply one of the strangest things I've ever encountered on this job."

"You mean, besides the head you found spiked to the *Wall Street Bull* or the vampire cult we uncovered last year?"

"Well, this *is* New York, isn't it?"

Martelli picked up his telephone headset, hit the speakerphone button so O'Keeffe could hear both sides of the call, and using the keypad, punched in Missy Dugan's extension.

"Well, well, well, if it isn't Louis Martelli . . . the man, the myth, the legend! Wazup, Lou?"

"Do me a big favor. Go into the computerized archives for all of the newspapers published in and around Syracuse between, say, 1993 and 1995, inclusive, and copy every article you can find in the news and sports sections having to do with our vic, Trent Morrison. Also take a look at what was going on with the football team at Marquis de La Fayette High School."

"I can do that. But is there anything specific you're looking for, Lou?"

"Yeah, I really want to know what made him turn to drugs in his junior year. The guy apparently was an honor student. Yes, I know, I know . . . kids experiment with drugs and alcohol. The fact his problem was bad enough for him to go through rehab as a teenager tells me there must be more to the story than we're seeing. In short, I want to know what triggered his problem."

"Got it!"

"While you're working that angle, Sean and I are going to run up to Bernstein, Fallen & Mark and see what we can learn."

■ *Theodore Jerome Cohen*

Ten

'**Ms.** Fallen will see you now, gentlemen. Please follow me." Martelli and O'Keeffe rose from their chairs in the waiting room of Bernstein, Fallen & Mark, and followed Isabella, the founder's administrative assistant, through the double-glass doors to a wood-paneled office in the back of the law office's suite on Park Avenue.

Fallen stood as they entered her office. "Gentlemen, please come in."

Marie Fallen was a woman in her early 50s. Born and raised in Chicago and a graduate of the University of Pennsylvania Wharton School, she earned her stripes in the rough and tumble trading pits of the Chicago Mercantile Exchange, where she specialized in hog and cattle futures. When two other traders, Joel Bernstein, who specialized in financial instruments, and Kenneth Mark, who specialized in currencies, asked her to join them in opening a new corporation in New York City, she packed her bags and never looked back.

She motioned for them to sit at the circular table to one end of her office. "May I offer you coffee? Tea? A soft drink, perhaps?"

"Nothing for me, thanks. Sean?"

"A cup of coffee would be great, thanks."

"Cream and sugar, Detective?" asked Isabella, as she went to pour a cup of coffee from the elegant silver coffee pot on the credenza.

"Black is fine, thanks."

She handed the cup and saucer to O'Keeffe.

"Will there be anything else, Ms. Fallen?"

"No, Isabella. Thank you. Please hold my calls."

Once Isabella had left the room, Fallen turned her attention to Martelli and O'Keeffe. "So, how can I help you?"

"We'd like to ask you just a few questions about Trent Morrison, Ms. Fallen."

"Oh, yes. Simply awful what happened. It will leave a big hole in our operation. He was a rising star, you know. Keen mind. Quick to act. He knew the markets and how they behaved. I personally will miss him as a professional and a friend."

Martelli took out his notepad. "When was the last time you saw Mr. Morrison?"

"That would have been the day he died. He was in the office the entire day. We were quite busy. I saw him on the trading floor several times, including during lunch."

"Did you talk with him at any point during the day?"

Fallen thought for a few seconds. "Let's see . . . we discussed some currency trades—hedges—he executed on behalf of two overseas clients, but nothing out of the ordinary."

"How was he behaving?"

"He was harried, but that wasn't unusual. When the commodity markets are open, tension is high. I'm sure you've seen pictures of the futures trading pits and all the yelling that goes on. Trading commodity futures is a blood sport, Detective, believe me. And Trent, being an old quarterback, loved to mix it up with the best of them. He—"

O'Keeffe interrupted here. "We understand he was quite the athlete. Did he ever talk about his old high school days in general or his junior and senior years as a quarterback in particular?"

"Only during the professional football season. We'd sometimes get together at my home during the fall and winter to watch the pros play. Every once in a while he'd see a play that would remind him of something from his days in high school. Apparently he and two other students—they were called The Flying Horsemen—really tore up the competition on many occasions. They took the team to two successive division championships, you know.

45

"Trent once told me fans called them The Flying Horsemen because their successes reminded some of the dramatic accomplishments achieved on the field by the Four Horsemen of Notre Dame. Those three boys—Trent and his friends—absolutely loved being compared to members of the famed 1924 team under Knute Rockne. Trent said he liked nothing better than to hear someone mention his name and that of Notre Dame's quarterback Harry Stuhldreher in the same sentence."

Martelli nodded. "That's very interesting. You wouldn't happen to know the names of the other two players, by chance?"

"Not off hand, Detective. But come to think of it, he kept a picture of the three of them on the credenza in his office. And each had signed the photo. I'm sure it's still there. We haven't packed his things yet. Would you care to walk down the hall? We could take a look?"

"Yes, we'd like that. But before we go, I have one more question, Ms. Fallen. During your last few encounters with Mr. Morrison, how would you describe his demeanor, other than the fact he appeared to be working under pressure?"

"He seemed in great spirits, Detective. He was directing his two traders, just as he always did, occasionally interjecting a joke at the expense of our clients. I'd say he was at the top of his game and thoroughly enjoying what the markets were throwing at him. He was a professional, through and through."

O'Keeffe picked up the conversation here. "So, as far as you could see, he wasn't distracted by anything. More to the point, to the best of your knowledge, he certainly didn't seem like the kind of person who would go home and overdose on heroin that evening."

"Heavens no, Detective! I think that would have been the last thing on his mind. Why, I can't even believe he used drugs. There never once was any indication he abused anything . . . drugs or alcohol.

"Why are you asking these questions? It sounds as if he didn't take his own life, as if this really is a case of murder!"

Fallen's no fool, thought Martelli. "I'm sure you can understand in a case like this, we have to cover all the bases. You're certainly not the first person who has told us Mr. Morrison's demeanor was far from that of someone who was suicidal on the day of this death. And yet, people's circumstances can change in an instant for reasons none of us can fathom. We want to make sure we run every possibility to ground before the coroner signs off on the death certificate."

"I understand, Detective.

"So, if we're done here, would you like to see his office?"

"We'll follow you," said Martelli as they rose.

Martelli and O'Keeffe followed Fallen out of her office and down the hall two doors to Morrison's office, a suite almost as large as Fallen's. One wall was covered with computer monitors that even in his absence were displaying commodity

47

prices in multi-color displays at a pace that made the wall look like a Christmas tree festooned with thousands of blinking lights.

As Fallen had said, a framed, autographed picture of The Flying Horsemen in their uniforms was on the credenza immediately behind Morrison's swivel chair. In the picture were Morrison, the quarterback, Brian Hallaway, a wide receiver, and Dan Chapman, a fullback. On each side of the photograph were the Horsemen's football records for their junior and senior years. Together, they had rolled up more yardage, wins, and awards for the school than had ever been achieved before or after their reign. In a word, the trio had been 'unstoppable.'

Martelli took the picture from the shelf. "Do you think your assistant would mind making a copy for us before we leave? It might at some point prove helpful in our investigation."

"Of course, let's take it with us. I'll have Isabella make a copy on our way out. Is there anything else you need?"

"Not right now, but if something comes to mind, we'll be in touch."

The men walked down the hall to Isabella's desk, where they bid goodbye to Fallen.

Once they had secured a copy of the photograph, Isabella signed them out at the front desk, and the men left the building.

On their way back to the First Precinct, Martelli called the IT Lab. "Missy, I've got two names for you: Brian Hallaway and

Dan Chapman. If it's any help, they played football with Morrison in the same timeframe you're using for that search I gave you earlier. See if you can learn anything about them. What happened to them after high school, where did they go, where are they now, what are they doing?"

"Brian Hallaway? He's dead, Lou. The guy overdosed on heroin two years ago."

Martelli jerked the steering wheel hard-left, executed an illegal U-turn in the middle of the block—which startled O'Keeffe, who was staring at a curvaceous blond in a tight skirt attempt to untangle her dog's leash as she tried to walk him across the street—and headed his *Crown Vic* toward 1PP. "We're on our way to your lab now."

■ *Theodore Jerome Cohen*

<u>Eleven</u>

"Talk to me, Missy." Martelli and O'Keeffe had been on their way back to the First Precinct when Dugan, who had been investigating Trent Morrison's high school years, startled the pair by announcing another of The Flying Horsemen had been found dead of a heroin overdose some years earlier. "How did you learn about Brian Hathaway's death?"

"Lou, this tale would put Shakespeare to shame. Talk about a tangled web. Morrison, Hallaway, and Chapman may have been heroes on the gridiron, but off the field, they were hellions of the worst kind. I barely scratched the surface of the newspaper archives you asked me to retrieve when I started finding stories about how the three of them were repeatedly cited by the local authorities for various infractions. They were mostly minor at first—a little underage drinking, some vandalism, and the like—but as time wore on, things went south fast, with some serious fender-benders, fist-fights, and one no-holds-barred, knock-down-drag-out fight on another high school team's turf."

Lou nodded. "Sounds like it got ugly."

"Oh, yeah, that it did. But given the football culture of the town and the wealth of the families involved, their parents were able to keep a lid on things when it came to the police and the courts."

O'Keeffe shrugged. "So far it sounds pretty much like a lot of what you read about in these small towns, where everything revolves around football. I don't see anything here that would lay the groundwork for murder."

"Well, I haven't told you the best—or perhaps, the worst—part yet. So, you may want to reserve judgment for now."

Dugan flipped through some copies of newspaper clippings she had printed until she found the one for which she was looking. "Here it is. It's not pretty. On Friday night, October 21, 1994, Marquis de La Fayette High School trounced its rival by a blowout score of 56 to 0. It was a total rout, Lou. After the game, the team and cheerleaders drove out to one of the player's homes to celebrate. The parents weren't home, and as you can imagine, everyone got pretty sloshed. More importantly, quite of few of the ladies favored the young lads with their presence in bed, with all but one going willingly. And that's when things turned really brutal."

"Let me guess," said Martelli. "Someone cried rape."

"Actually, gang rape . . . by The Flying Horsemen. Her name was Emily Thompson, a straight-A honor student. Not only did her parents charge Morrison, Hallaway, and Chapman with rape on her behalf, but they also charged them with taking pictures of her assault and rape and of distributing them around their high school.

"Now, even though this was in the days before cyberbullying, the impact was horrific. Thompson was harassed constantly, and whether in school or on the street, she was called a slut, skag, and whore, among other names . . . and that was coming just from the girls in her school."

"My father always used to tell me, teenage girls, he said, are the true pornographers in our society."

"And just how did he come to that stunning conclusion, Lou?"

Martelli laughed. "Back in the '50s he worked part-time as a janitor in the old Avon Theater that used to stand on 9th Street between 4th and 5th Avenues in Park Slope. You know, those were the days when neighborhood theaters ran a double feature, several cartoons, a movie serial, and a newsreel, all for a pittance. Anyway, he said what the girls used to write and draw on the mirrors over the sinks in the lavatories with their lipsticks would make Hugh Hefner blush."

Dugan didn't skip a beat. "Well, I can tell you from personal experience, when it comes to being bitchy, teenage girls have no equal. Boys couldn't hold a candle to them.

"Anyway, Lou, in Emily's case, the town sided with the boys—their star players on the gridiron. Two weeks after her parents filed charges, Thompson hung herself in the girl's locker room at the school."

No one said anything for a few seconds. Finally, Martelli, who appeared to be thinking about his teenage daughter, spoke. "What happened then?"

53

"There were the usual formal inquiries, as you might expect . . . and the usual conflicting stories and questions as to exactly what happened that evening. Was the sex consensual? Some said 'yes,' some said 'no.' Was the girl being flirtatious? Some said 'yes,' some said 'no.' Was money changing hands to keep things quiet and out of the courts? Always a possibility.

"In the end, the case was dropped, the team went on to win the division championship, The Flying Horsemen graduated with their class in June the following year, and at least until now, that appeared to be the end of the story."

Martelli shook his head. There was no question he was disgusted by what Dugan had told him. "Well, if my hunch is correct, someone just reopened the case and took vengeance on Morrison in the process. I'm wondering, too, if he's actually the second in line for such punishment, with Hallaway having already paid his dues.

"Where did Hallaway die, Missy?"

"In an old industrial section of Syracuse. He was homeless. After high school, he enlisted in the Army and served several tours with the 10th Mountain Division, a light infantry division, in Iraq and Afghanistan. After separating from the service, he returned to northern New York and worked in law enforcement for a while. But his post-traumatic stress disorder got worse, and he couldn't hold a job. He finally ended up on the street and was found dead of a heroin overdose just before Thanksgiving, 2011."

"Can I use your phone?"

"Of course."

Martelli picked up the handset, hit the 'Speakerphone' button, and punched up Antonetti's extension.

The deputy coroner answered after one ring. "Yes, Missy."

"Michael, it's Louis. Would you please call the medical examiner in Syracuse and ask him if his office performed an autopsy on one Brian Hallaway? The man overdosed on heroin just before Thanksgiving in 2011. He was a close friend of our vic Morrison, and he may have died under similar circumstances. If an autopsy was performed, see if he'll release a copy to you."

"What else do I need to know?" asked Antonetti, concerned about walking into a buzz saw.

"If the coroner starts asking questions, just say we're investigating what appears to be an accidental heroin overdose of a man who was a close friend of Hallaway's, and we're just trying to connect the dots. I don't want to stir up a hornet's nest up there, but the fact is, your call is a prelude to our going to our asking for an order to exhume Hallaway's body."

"Okay, Louis. This is indeed a delicate situation. If Hallaway's accidental death turns out to be murder, the medical examiner in Syracuse might be very embarrassed. We have to handle this *very* carefully and make sure the ME is protected. But we've been through this kind of thing before with the Lake George's Sheriff Office, remember? Trust me. I'll take care of it."

"I'm counting on it. Bye."

Martelli set the telephone headset in its cradle.

"Before we go, Missy, is there anything you can tell us about Chapman."

"Not this minute, but I'm still digging."

Twelve

As Martelli and O'Keeffe were leaving the basement of 1PP, they chanced to pass the Evidence Room. "Sean, hold up a second. I want to confirm something that's been bothering me."

It didn't take but a few minutes before the clerk brought the Morrison evidence box to the counter. Martelli signed for it, and the men retired to a cubicle on one side of the room.

"Whadja have in mind, Lou?"

"Remember how Morrison's housekeeper said the front door was locked from the inside when she arrived. There were two locks on that door, one of them being a bolt lock. If Morrison locked that door after his visitor left, then his key should still be in his possession. However, if the killer took his key and used it to lock the door *from the outside,* then we should not find a house key among Morrison's effects."

"Well, here's the key you took from the housekeeper."

Sean handed him the clear plastic envelope containing the key that worked on both door locks.

Search as they might, they could not find a similar key among the other items in the evidence box, not even among those on Morrison's key ring.

"Sean, I don't think there's any question the perp took the house key from the vic's key ring and used it to lock the doors to the townhouse on her way out. But I doubt she'd be so foolish as to discard it in the curb. Just the same, have a black and white check the area ASAP."

Thirteen

'Doctor Fitzpatrick, my name is Dr. Antonetti, Michael Antonetti. I'm a deputy coroner with the New York Police Department. How are you today?"

Dillon Fitzpatrick, MD, was the medical examiner for the Onondaga County Health Department. A trained forensic pathologist, his geographical area of responsibility included the city of Syracuse, NY. A gentleman in his early 60s, he had held the office for more than 30 years and was well respected both among his peers and the citizens of the county. The work he performed was similar to that of a coroner . . . investigating deaths and injuries that occurred under suspicious circumstances, conducting autopsies, determining the cause of death, issuing death certificates, and the like.

"Good afternoon, Michael. And please call me Dillon. How can I help you?"

"Dillon, we have an unusual situation down here that may or may not be connected with a case you handled some years ago. I thought I'd run a few things by you in the hope you might be able to help us."

"Of course. I'll do whatever I can."

"Well, some of what I'm going to tell you hasn't been released to the public, so I'd appreciate it if you'd keep it close to your vest for now. But as you may know, Brian Morrison was found dead in his apartment earlier this week. You probably remember the man from his high school days in your area."

"Oh yes, no question about that. He was quite the football star. And I did see something in our local paper about his death, an accidental drug overdose, I believe. There wasn't much information in the article, but from what I read, he appeared to overdose on heroin, with alcohol a contributing factor. Did you find evidence of foul play?"

"In a word, yes. I performed an autopsy on Morrison yesterday, and let's just say I found some things to suggest he may not have been alone when he died. Now, whether or not the person or persons with him were complicit in his death is a matter still to be determined. But the fact is, it's an open case at this time and two of our detectives are pursuing it with all urgency."

"I understand, Michael, but I don't see how I can help you. Morrison left the area years ago. In fact, the last time most people from around here saw him was when he played football in his senior year at that private high school he attended south of town."

"Yes, of course. But the thing we found interesting, Dillon, is that another of his teammates, Brian Hallaway, also apparently died of a heroin overdose compounded by alcohol. Do you recall that case?"

"Oh, yes, that was tragic. Another member of The Flying Horsemen. He came back a changed man after serving in the military ... started drinking, doing drugs, couldn't hold a job. Lived with his parents for a while until they threw him out. He was in and out of rehab several times, but even the VA couldn't help him, and he ended up on the street. I understand he was in and out of the emergency room at the local hospital at least three times in the two months before he died, so nobody was surprised when they found him dead in an alley one morning of an overdose."

"Did they bring him to your morgue after he was found?"

"Yes, of course. Under the circumstances, we had to rule out foul play."

"And so, you performed an autopsy?"

"Absolutely. Given where he was found, it was incumbent on me to know exactly how he died. I must say, however, it wasn't difficult to come to a determination."

"Why was that?"

"Well, for one thing, his blood-alcohol level was through the roof. And when you add in the other results of the tox screen, which showed excessively high levels of pure heroin in his body, there simply was no other conclusion one could draw. The man fell asleep and forgot to breathe!"

"So, the cause of death was listed as—?"

"Drug overdose compounded by high levels of alcohol in his the bloodstream."

"If I e-mailed you a formal request, might it be possible to obtain a copy of your report?"

"Of course. You have my phone number, so I assume you also found my e-mail address."

"Oh, yes. By the way, I should tell you there is the possibility our people might be calling for the exhumation of Hallaway's body."

"What? Why would you do that? You haven't even seen my autopsy report yet!"

Antonetti tried to calm the waters. "I know, I know, and frankly, though I can't discuss the details with you now, this has nothing whatsoever to do with your autopsy and more to do with some people down here covering their collective assess, if you catch my drift.

"Frankly, we—you and me, Dillon—have a bad situation here. We have these two men—Morrison and Hallaway—who not only were close friends but who apparently died under similar if not identical circumstances. For all intents and purposes, both of their deaths look accidental.

"But some things simply don't add up on Morrison's death, Dillon, and so, I've had to put off signing his death certificate. This has *not* made my boss happy, believe me, especially with the press nipping at his heels."

"I'm beginning to understand the problem, Michael."

"Can you imagine the howl that will go up, Dillon, if Morrison's death is proven to be murder and the press starts digging into Hallaway's case? It won't be that difficult for them to put 2 and 2 together, given the men's high school history."

"Michael, I have an idea. Why don't *I* call for an exhumation of Hallaway's body based on the fact that Morrison died under similar circumstances? And just to ensure impartiality, I'll request that a second, independent autopsy be performed by the NYPD coroner's office. Would that be something your office could handle?"

"Most assuredly. Coordinate everything with me. In fact, I will make sure that the Coroner's Office assigns the case to me. But I'll leave it to you to work with the Hallaway family. Under the circumstances, I'm sure they would want to know what happened to their son. And Dillon . . . thank you so much."

"Thank *you,* Michael. I'm up for reappointment in 2014. The last thing I need is a scandal."

■ *Theodore Jerome Cohen*

Fourteen

"**W**ell, well, if it isn't Mrs. Martelli's *wunderkind*, detective-inspector Louis Martelli!" Dugan didn't even have to look up from her workbench, knowing as she did the sounds of Martelli's distinctive footsteps from years of hearing the man enter her lab in search of help on his case *de jour.* "What happened, did you get tired of flexing your muscles for the chicks in tight spandex pants at the Dominant Fitness & Health Club? Or did they laugh you out of the place?"

Martelli worked hard to keep his weight down, primarily to ease the burden on his legs. But at 6-foot, 2-inches and 190 pounds, walking with a prosthesis could still be difficult at times. This was one of his main reasons for working out every weekday morning before driving into the city from Brooklyn to begin work.

"Wow, from the looks of the place, Dugan, don't you think it's time to call someone in to help you repair whatever it is you've managed to screw up? And so early in the day, too. Only 7:15 in the morning, and if I had to guess, the entire NYPD e-mail system must be down!"
It wasn't quite as bad as Martelli made it out to be, though he was closer than he knew to the truth. The primary e-mail

server for the entire Department had indeed failed during the night. However, with the usual automatic failover capability in place, the backup e-mail server took over in a fraction of a second, and there was no noticeable impact on users. Now, Dugan had pulled the faulty server to her bench, and after disassembling it, was in the process of troubleshooting the unit.

"Actually, you're not as dumb as you look, Martelli. The primary e-mail server *did* go down last night, and while it would be easy to simply replace a faulty board, I love a challenge . . . hence I'm trying to track down the fault. The IT tech couldn't get here until 8 AM, anyway, so at the very least, it's good practice."

She continued to probe various boards with her test equipment, stopping every once in a while to compare the readings on her multimeter with the values specified on the schematics in the server's technical manual.

"May I ask you a question while you work on that board?"

"Sure. Shoot!"

"Were you able to find out anything about the third Flying Horsemen, that guy Dan Chapman?"

"Yeah, I found him. It was easy."

"How'd you do that?"
"I called his mother in Nedrow, New York. Told her I was with the government, mentioned that the New York State

Comptroller in Albany has unclaimed property for her son, and indicated we needed to get in touch with him."

"You *what?*"

Martelli was almost apoplectic. "You called his mother and lied to her? You can't do that, Dugan!"

"Don't get your panties in a twist, Martelli! I didn't lie to her. What part of 'I'm with the government' and 'the New York State Comptroller in Albany has unclaimed property for her son' isn't true? I checked. The Comptroller *does* have funds waiting up there . . . at least, someone with the name 'Dan Chapman' has funds waiting to be retrieved."

"But it was a total subterfuge meant to obtain information under false pretenses," Martelli sputtered.

"Oh, oh, look who's talking, the high and mighty Detective-Inspector Louis Martelli, defender of all that is moral and ethical. As I recall, it was one Louis Martelli who whined, begged, and pleaded with his partner in crime, the beautiful, highly intelligent NYPD Principal Information Technology Specialist Missy Dugan, until said specialist finally agreed to hack into the FBI's secure server in Quantico, Virginia a year or so ago and download everything belonging to that agency's special agent in charge of the New York Field Office. Did I miss anything?"

"That was a unique situation Missy, and you know it! Besides, Agent Ron Bishop wasn't sharing information with me on the death of that Wall Street banker and those who may have been involved in his murder. I don't have any regrets about what we did. What we did helped to solve the case."

The room was silent for a minute as Dugan continued probing the server's various printed-circuit boards.

"Ah-ha, here's the problem . . . the low-voltage power supply board will have to be replaced. All the voltages are out of spec. The service tech can swap boards in a flash when he gets here, so we should have this puppy back on line in no time.

"I'd fix the board myself, Lou, but the service agent goes crazy and starts making noise about voiding the warranty and shit like that. Fine! The first time he fails to produce someone to service one of our systems within the time frame specified by the warranty, I'll make him eat the damn piece of paper."

Martelli appeared to have settled down. "Well, okay. I guess you found the solution to your problem. Good work. I'm impressed. So, are you going to give me Chapman's contact information?"

"Sorry, Lou, no can do. And believe me, I'd love to give it to you. I know it would be of immense help to you on this case. But knowingly giving you information acquired under false pretenses would prevent you from claiming plausible deniability when they put you on the stand at my trial, and I couldn't let that happen."

Martelli's face turned a bright red. "Are you shitting me? I need to get in touch with his guy. His life might be in danger. Give me the goddamn information, Missy."

"Well, now that you put it that way, I'm going to write his contact information on a piece of paper and leave it on my workbench. And if by chance someone picks it up, there's nothing I can do about it."

Dugan accessed her desk phone's console for the information and wrote three telephone numbers on a small piece of paper—Chapman's office number and his business and private cell phone numbers. Ever so slowly she edged the paper toward Martelli, who snatched it from the workbench in a flourish.

"By the way," Dugan continued, "Chapman works for an ad agency on Madison Avenue. But you won't be able to reach him right now. He's out of the country. I know because I called his office, speaking as a government representative, of course. He won't be back for several days, maybe a week. They weren't sure."

"You're going to be the death of me yet."

■ *Theodore Jerome Cohen*

Fifteen

'P'ack your bags, Sean. We're going back to high school."
Martelli had just left the IT Lab and was heading back
to his office in the First Precinct. "Captain Hanlon
agreed we need to extend this investigation into the Syracuse
area."

"I thought you wanted to get in touch with Dan Chapman in
the worse way, Lou. This is hardly the time to leave town with
one of the three Horsemen still standing."

"I agree, except Chapman is out of the country, and I'd have
to assume safe for now. And given the fact we're waiting on
the exhumation of Brian Hallaway's body and Michael's
autopsy of that body—though after all these years, God knows
what he'll be able to determine—this would be a good time to
see what we can learn up in Syracuse about The Flying
Horsemen and Emily Thompson. I'm hoping that somewhere
in that story we'll find a lead to whoever is avenging her
death."

"Okay, I'll go home, pack, gas up my car, and pick you up at
your place in an hour or so."

"Whoa, good buddy, not so fast. I'm driving this time."

"What's the matter, you don't like the way I drive?"

"No, it's not that at all. The New York State Police don't like the way you drive. Or did you forget our last trip, the one to Lake George?"

A year earlier, on their way from Manhattan to Lake George, NY with O'Keeffe at the wheel, he was clocked doing more than 100 miles per hour on I-81 N before being pulled over by a state trooper. When the trooper, Logan by name, sarcastically told O'Keeffe that he had spent the last two hours behind a clump of trees just waiting for him to drive by, O'Keeffe's nonplussed response was, 'Well, Sergeant, I got here as quickly as I could.' Martelli was sure they would end up in front of a magistrate in some jerkwater town and have to pay a fine. Fortunately, the trooper had a good sense of humor and let the pair off with the suggestion O'Keeffe might want to keep it under 80.

"Just go home and pack, Sean. I'll be by in an hour to pick *you* up. Plan on spending at least two days in the Syracuse area. I'll take care of our motel reservations."

Sixteen

The trip to Syracuse took a little over four hours, including one 'pit stop' for gas and a bathroom break. Along the way, the men talked about many things, ranging from the current case, to Sean's wedding plans, to their time in the Army. Of course, the conversation was punctuated with the usual good humor and verbal sparring that always had marked their relationship and helped them through the bad times together.

"Better watch out here, Lou," O'Keeffe warned as they neared the spot on I-81 N where they had been pulled over on their previous trip north. "I'm sure Sergeant Logan is just itching to get his hands on you. Oh, wait . . . I think I see him behind that clump of trees."

Instinctively, Martelli took his foot off the accelerator, letting the *Crown Vic* drift ever so slowly from 85 to 75 miles per hour.

O'Keeffe chuckled.

"I'm not tempting fate, Sean. With you in the car, lightning is sure to strike twice! And the last thing we need is to be hauled up in front of a magistrate. Captain Hanlon would have kittens, and we'd be the laughingstock of the precinct."

No sooner had he said that when his cell phone rang. It was Antonetti.

"Yeah, Michael. Waddaya got?"

"Louis, good news. Hallaway's body is being exhumed as we speak. I've sent Williams up to Onondaga County with a van and driver to pick up the casket. She should be back tonight, and I'll begin work early tomorrow morning.

"Frankly, I've read the coroner's report. It looks pretty thorough. It should. The guy's a forensic pathologist. Anyway, the tox screen certainly supports a determination of death by drug overdose compounded by high levels of alcohol ingestion.

"To tell the truth, Louis, I'm not sure what more we're going to learn beyond what's already in the ME's report. The body's been in the ground for two years, and the internal organs, what remains of them, have no doubt deteriorated. But we'll see. The viscera bag will either be sewn into the body or found at the foot end of the casket. It won't be difficult to find."

Martelli chuckled. "Now I know why I never look at the deceased's shoes at a funeral."

"Well, in cases such as this, please keep in mind the state of preservation varies greatly, and whether or not we'll even be able to run valid tox screens depends upon a number of factors, not the least of which is the length of time the body has been in the ground. But autolysis and putrefaction begins immediately after death, and they simply continue along Nature's predetermined timetable."

Martelli said nothing.

"Why do I get the feeling you aren't all that concerned about a second autopsy, Louis?"

Martelli laughed. "All right, I plead guilty. What I really want is to get my hands on the body *and* the casket. The thought occurred to me that if Hallaway was indeed murdered, the killer may have left a calling card as they did in Morrison's case. Remember the case we worked on two years ago in which the killer, a member of a vampire cult, stuffed garlic in his victims' mouths at their funerals?"

"Yes, of course. That was pretty macabre. Do you think we'll find a coin in Hallaway's mouth?"

"Whether we find it in his mouth—perhaps put there at the time of the murder or at the funeral—is yet to be determined. But it's worth a look.

"As well, Michael, I want the people in CSU to go over every inch of the casket before you even touch the body. I'll make arrangements for that. I have to call over there anyway."

"I understand. Okay, it's your show. I'll stand by until I hear from CSU. Bye."

Martelli ended the call, and with a few deft thumb strokes, called NYPD's Crime Scene Unit.

"NYPD CSU, Sergeant Reynolds."

"Hey, Adam, how ya doin', man?"

Reynolds voice brightened when he heard Lou's. "Hey, Lou! I've been waiting for your call. That coin you asked us to look at, the one Antonetti sent over on the Morrison case . . . I'm sorry, but there wasn't even the hint of a fingerprint on the coin."

"That's okay, I understand. Did you find anything at the Morrison townhouse, anything at all?"

"Naw, the place was clean. The only prints we lifted belonged to him and the housekeeper. If anyone was with him on the night he died, they didn't leave a trace. Believe me, if they had, my people would have found it."

Martelli pursed his lips and shook his head. "Damn! I was really hoping we'd at least find a partial print—something on a glass or in the bathroom—or maybe even a hair."

"Did Antonetti find anything on the body when he did his external examination?

"No, he did a thorough check even before the body was moved . . . you know, the vic's hands, face, clothing, the position of the body, and so forth. Yes, it looked like he had overdosed, but Antonetti found things that didn't add up. The tie-off used to raise the vein in his arm was in the wrong place and, according to Michael, possibly on the wrong arm. Which is why he thinks the vic may not have died of an accidental overdose and why Sean and I are running all over hell and gone in search of a killer."

"Well, you know we'll do whatever we can to help."

"Along those lines, Adam, we're having another body exhumed today in upstate New York . . . a friend of the vic who, interestingly, also died of a drug overdose a while back. Antonetti's sent a van for the casket, and he should have it sometime tonight. I'd like your people to go over it *and* the body with a fine-tooth comb before Antonetti does his thing. Can you bump these things to the top of your list?"

"It'll be tight, Lou, but I'll contact Michael now and make the arrangements."

"Thanks. I knew I could count on you. We'll talk later!"

"Right. Best to Stephanie."

"And to yours, as well."

Martelli ended the call and placed his phone on the seat beside him.

The men pressed on toward Syracuse.

"So, Lou, how's the family?"

"We're well, thanks. Biggest problem is keeping the kids on the straight and narrow. I'll tell you, Sean, all this crap with social media—Facebook, Twitter, and the like—it's enough to drive Steph and me into an early grave. We've had to place severe limits on the kids' use of their computers and mobile devices. I mean, how much of that can a parent put up with in a day?"

Sean laughed. "I guess every time someone farts, tries a new brand of nail polish, and takes a selfie, people today have to telegraph the news to their 'followers.'" He formed quotation marks using his fingers.

"The abuse of cell phone cameras is the worst. I've warned Tiffany in particular about this."

"I hear you. Did you see that case in the paper about the 18-year-old guy who posted a picture online of him and his nude 16-year-old girlfriend doing the deed? He posted the picture as revenge for her jilting him?"

Martelli laughed. "Oh, yeah. The guy's fucked! Not only was he found guilty in federal court of possessing kiddie porn, but now, he'll have to register as a sex offender . . . for the rest of his life. That's going to make a great impression on future employers, assuming he can even get a job. I love it. US Code Title 18 Chapter 110, one of my all-time favorites."

"Actions have consequences. Kids today don't think about that. It's like, 'Hey, wouldn't this be awesome?!' Consequences? What are those?"

"Well, if I've told Tiffany and Rob once I've told them a thousand times, even a fish wouldn't get caught if he kept his mouth shut."

Sean nodded. "Yes, that, and never put anything in writing."

Seventeen

'I know it's getting late, Sean, but let's take a chance and see if we can catch the principal at that private school where The Flying Horsemen left their mark. We have our motel reservations, so checking in late is not a problem."

The Marquis de La Fayette High School was a prestigious, private, co-ed educational institution located on 25 lush acres just to the south of Syracuse, NY. It drew students from all over the US, though most were drawn from wealthier families in New England in general and New York in particular. The school offered a broad variety of academic and sports programs, and it was well recognized for excellence in both. The school's alumni included many well-recognized members of the scientific, legal, and business professions, and through them, the school enjoyed one of the largest endowments of any institution of its kind in the US.

The principal, Edward Lane, had been with the school since 1993, first as a science teacher, and then, in 2007, as its principal. He graciously made time to see Martelli and O'Keeffe as the school day drew to a close.

"Gentlemen, come in, come in. I apologize in advance for the appearance of my office. Things get a little hectic around here."

"You should see Detective Martelli's office, sir. Compared to yours, his looks like a F5 tornado went through it!"

They shared a good laugh, and sat, Lane behind his desk, the two detectives in front of it.

"Oh, excuse my manners," apologized Lane. "Would either of you care for something to drink?"

"A cold glass of water is all I need," responded Martelli.

O'Keeffe requested a cold soft drink.

Lane picked up his telephone's headset, dialed 0, and when his secretary picked up her phone, he requested the refreshments.

"Now, how can I help you?"

Martelli led off the conversation. "Ed, we're investigating what appears to be the suicide of a former student at this school. The victim's name was Trent Morrison. Does he ring a bell?"

"Oh, heavens yes, Trent, I remember him, one of the fabled Flying Horsemen. Man, you should have—"

There was a knock at the door.

"Come in, Dorothy."

Lane's secretary entered, carrying a tray on which was Martelli's glass of water and a can of soda together with a glass filled with ice cubes. She set the tray on the desk in front of the men.

Lane thanked her, whereupon she turned and left the room, shutting the door behind her.

"As I was saying, you should have seen those three boys play football. There was never anything like them before *or* after they were here. Trent's junior and senior years—he was the quarterback, you know—were simply remarkable when it came to our football team's ability to rack up scores, records, and championships."

Both Martelli and O'Keeffe were furiously taking notes.

Martelli was the first to respond. "All this, of course, must have gone to their heads, to some extent. I mean, when teenagers achieve what Morrison, Hallaway, and Chapman did, they begin to feel special, even entitled, like the rules others are required to follow simply don't apply to them. There must have been consequences."

"Oh, indeed there were, Detective. It began in the fall of their junior year, after the team started off to a great season. At first it manifested itself in the form of classroom discipline problems, but soon, we were seeing other issues . . . drinking, some drug use—mostly marijuana—drag racing, and the like. The problems continued after the football season was over, and as I'm sure you know—and this certainly isn't telling tales out of school, as it were—Trent spent two months in alcohol

81

rehab during the summer between his junior and senior years. It was a well-known fact around here, to be sure, and even though he was a minor, the story appeared in at least one local newspaper."

O'Keeffe's ears perked up on this. "Is there any chance you kept a copy of that or any other articles pertaining to Mr. Morrison or any other member of The Flying Horsemen?"

"I'm afraid not, Detective. That was a long time ago, and I'm sure you can appreciate the fact there's only so much clutter an office can withstand before it collapses under its own weight."

O'Keeffe laughed. "Oh, yes, and we're still attempting to determine the critical load-bearing capacity for Lou's."

Martelli picked up the conversation. "What happened in their senior year, the second of the two great seasons?"

Lane shook his head. "That's when all hell broke loose. The team played even better than the year before. There was no stopping them now. Everyone was behind them . . . the students, the parents, the local community. They could do no wrong. And the more successful they were, the more they misbehaved. Now, the criminal misconduct escalated. Their drug and alcohol use became more rampant, as did the drag racing. There were a number of serious accidents, in fact, with several students ending up in the hospital on more than a few occasions. But the greatest tragedy of all occurred after one of the team's best games, a real blowout – 56 to 0 against our greatest rival—a humiliating defeat, to be sure.

"After the game, the entire team, including the cheerleaders, gathered at the home of one of our students. The only problem was, the parents weren't home. Neighbors finally called the police but not before the students had done more than $10,000 damage to the house and its furnishings."

O'Keeffe interrupted him. "And that's where Emily Thompson claims she was raped by The Flying Horsemen."

"Yes. But she didn't come forward right away. Even after some students distributed pictures of the assaults and rapes the following Monday, she kept silent. But after more than a week of being bullied in her classes and in the hallways—something the school tried to stop, believe me—her parents finally took her to the police and filed formal charges against the three boys."

"And the result was . . .?" asked Martelli.

"People rallied behind the three boys. Remember, this was one of those 'she said,' 'they said' situations. Emily never denied she was making out with one of the three boys in an upstairs bedroom—I recall she named Morrison—but claims when things started to heat up, she repeatedly told him to stop. Apparently, this only enraged him, and he became more aggressive.

"When Hallaway and Chapman joined them, it got worse. The commotion attracted others at the party, including some of Emily's girlfriends, who supported the fact she told the men to stop."

Martelli was scribbling as fast as he could. "Do you remember any of the girlfriends' names?"

Lane paused and pursed his lips. "It's been a while, but two come to mind. Joanne Baldwin and Kimberly Lathrope."

"Did anyone else hear her tell the boys to stop?"

Lane thought for a second. "Another of the team members apparently had come into the room when he heard all the yelling . . . Derek Hamilton. Now there was a gentleman, through and through. He came to her defense after she filed charges and some days later was found beaten behind the school. Fortunately, he recovered quickly."

"Did he name his attackers?"

"No, he refused. And no charges ever were filed."

O'Keeffe looked up from his notepad. "Where can we reach these three people?"

"I believe Joanne left the area for college and never returned. I have no idea where she is, though her parents may still be in the area.

"Kimberly still may live in upstate New York, but I haven't seen her since she was a student.

"Unfortunately, Derek Hamilton, who had been selected for promotion to lieutenant colonel last year, was killed in an ambush in Kandahar Province, Afghanistan, two months ago. I'll miss him. He was one of the school's best supporters.

Derek always came to speak to our students when he visited his folks up here. By the way, did you know he was the defensive team leader during the two seasons when The Flying Horsemen reigned? What a great player he was in his own right."

Martelli shook his head. He couldn't help but think about W.H. Auden's *Epitaph for an Unknown Soldier*. 'All gave some. Some gave all.'

O'Keeffe urged Lane to continue.

"There's not much more to say, gentlemen. Two weeks after the Thompsons filed charges against Morrison, Hallaway, and Chapman, the school janitor found Emily hanging from a shower head in the woman's locker room. The county coroner determined it was suicide, and she was buried in her church's cemetery. Hundreds attended the funeral.

"The district attorney opened an investigation in the matter, but the case against the three boys was dropped. The DA's belief was that despite the evidence, he didn't feel it would be possible to prove beyond a shadow of a doubt the sex was not consensual.

"And there the matter died. The three accused boys went on to graduate. Morrison went on to a career on Wall Street, Hallaway went into the Army, and Chapman ended up on Madison Avenue.

Lane paused, took a breath, and looked off into the far corner of his office. "Sad. Now two of the Horsemen are dead." He paused for a moment. "You *are* aware of what happened to Hallaway, right."

Martelli nodded. "We're aware of Mr. Hallaway's demise."

"What a pity. They all had such bright futures.

The detectives nodded.

"Well, I hope something I've told you will be of help in the Morrison case. It's been a while since anyone asked about The Flying Horsemen or Emily Thompson, God rest her soul."

The men stood. Martelli handed the principal his card. "You've been most helpful, Ed. If you happen to think of something we haven't touched on, please call me."

"I'll do that."

Eighteen

It was raining the following morning, a suitable prelude for meeting with the parents of Emily Thompson, the teenager who committed suicide after alleging she had been raped and bullied. There was no way, even on the sunniest of days, that a meeting to discuss a child's death could be anything but somber. *What could be worse than for a parent to bury their child?* thought Martelli.

The Thompson's home was a 5-bedroom, 4-bath, 5,000 square-foot brick colonial set back on four acres at the end of a long driveway in one of the more expensive suburbs south of Syracuse. Harold Thompson, Emily's father, had inherited a handsome sum of money from his father, who had made his money in the Great Lakes transportation industry, a business in which Harold had participated until selling out to a large European cartel in the 1980s. Since that time, Thompson had worked intermittently as a consultant to a limited number of international clients while his wife participated in various charitable organizations, both locally and in Washington, DC.

Martelli and O'Keeffe, as prearranged, drove to the house just before 9 AM and parked on the circle in front of the main entrance. Two gardeners were huddled in their truck. They were waiting patiently for the rain to stop so they could begin trimming the Japanese hollies bordering the front of the house and cutting the bright green grass that grew on the broad expanse of lawn to its front.

Patricia Thompson stood waiting at the door. She motioned for the men to come in.

Martelli and O'Keefe ran from the car to the house. Once inside, they brushed the rainwater off their suitcoats and introduced themselves.

Mrs. Thompson smiled, introduced herself, and stepped forward with two coat hangers. "Here, let me hang your jackets so they won't wrinkle."

The men took their cell phones, pens, and notebooks, and then, relinquished their jackets to Mrs. Thompson, who hung them in the hall closet.

"Now, please, come into the sitting room. I've had both coffee and tea prepared for you."

Harold Thompson was descending the large staircase opposite the front door as they began following Mrs. Thompson. "Good morning, Detectives. Welcome to our home." When he got to the bottom, the men shook hands, with Martelli and O'Keeffe giving the man their cards.

The three men joined Mrs. Thompson. "May I get you something, Detectives?"

"Coffee, black, please" responded Martelli.

O'Keeffe doubled the request.

The men sat while Mr. Thompson prepared the detectives' coffees.

Harold Thompson spoke first. "How can we help you, gentlemen? You indicated you had an interest in our daughter Emily's case. As you know, despite our best efforts and those of the police and the district attorney, the belief was it would have been highly unlikely a jury would have determined, beyond a shadow of a doubt, the sex was *not* consensual." He shook his head back and forth in despair and threw up his hands. "There was simply nothing we could do."

Thompson's voice started to crack and his eyes filled with tears. He turned away for a moment, composed himself, and then continued. "Those boys got off scot-free, went on to graduate high school, and moved on with their lives while we mourned the death of our only child."

Mrs. Thompson, who had been sitting next to your husband on an antique Louis XVI carved settee loveseat sofa, gently placed her hand on her husband's arm.

Mercifully, there was a knock at the door. Mr. Thompson responded: "Yes, Mary?"

The maid opened the door, and stepped inside. "I'm sorry to intrude, Mr. Thompson, but they are ready with your call from Dubai."

"Thank you, Mary. Please tell them I'll be there shortly." Mr. Thompson stood. "Patricia, Gentlemen, please excuse me. I'm sure my wife is more than able to answer your questions."

The detectives rose, shook his hand, and said their goodbyes.

Martelli leaned forward. "We are, of course, well acquainted with your daughter's case, Mrs. Thompson, and we extend our most sincere condolences.

"What brings us here today, however, is the hope that by talking with you, we will learn a little more about the events leading up to your daughter's death."

"I don't understand, Detective. Emily died so many years ago. Why would the New York Police Department be interested in her death now?"

"Well, Mrs. Thompson, as you may have read in your local papers, Trent Morrison recently was found dead in his Manhattan townhouse of an apparent suicide."

"Oh, yes, I did see something about that the other day. God forgive me, I can't say I'm sorry."

"Well, we're just trying to tie up some loose ends in that case. We know what happened between your daughter and Mr. Morrison when they were in high school together, and we want to rule out any connection between those unfortunate times and Mr. Morrison's recent death.

"More to the point, we hoped by talking to you, we might learn the names of your daughter's closest friends . . . the ones who would have been most affected by her death."

Martelli's comment caught Patricia Thompson by surprise. "Oh my God! Do you think one of my daughter's old friends might have avenged Emily's death by killing Mr. Morrison?"

O'Keeffe put his right hand up to calm her. "We don't know that, Mrs. Thompson. We'd just like to learn a little more about your daughter and her friends. Who were they? What they did and where they hung out during the last few months of Emily's life? These are the kind of questions we have today."

"Rather than answer them, Detectives, I'll take you to her room. It's exactly as it was the day she died. Perhaps if you looked around, you'll find the answers for yourselves."

■ *Theodore Jerome Cohen*

Nineteen

artelli and O'Keeffe followed Patricia Thompson up the long staircase to the home's second landing. From there, they turned to the right and walked down a long hall to the last door on the left.

"This is Emily's room. We haven't touched it. Mary cleans it once a week, but other than that, it's just the way she left it on the day—"

Mrs. Thompson hesitated. "On the day she died."

She opened the door and stepped aside so that Martelli and O'Keeffe could step inside. The room reminded Martelli a little of his own daughter's room with its shelves of stuffed animals, magazines lying here and there, and cosmetics strewn across the desk. It was the quintessential teenager's safe haven. Given its appearance, it seemed as if Emily had left for school just five minutes before the men arrived. Except she hadn't, and she never would return.

The way Martelli was looking around, it appeared he might have been thinking somewhere in that room was a clue that could help unravel the death of Trent Morrison and, perhaps, that of Brian Hallaway's as well. He donned latex gloves, as did O'Keeffe. Not that Emily's room was a crime scene. Still, if

93

the person avenging her death had been a close friend, then the possibility that person had been in Emily's bedroom was high.

Methodically the men began to go over the contents of the girl's bedroom. They studied the photographs on her desk and the room's walls, paged through the books on her shelves, flipped the pages of the magazines strewn around the room, and shuffled through the papers on her desk. A search of her drawers yielded a scattering of school assignments and notes but little of value. As necessary, they took photographs using the cameras in their cell phones.

It was O'Keeffe, standing on a chair and searching through the items stored on the shelf in the closet, who found the loose piece of wallboard sliced out of the closet wall. Behind it, standing on the closet wall's wood framing, was the girl's diary. Extracting it from its hiding place, O'Keeffe backed down off the chair and brought the leather-bound book to Martelli.

Patricia Thompson was surprised. "I never knew she was keeping a diary. She never mentioned it, and we never had discussed such a thing. May I have it?"

Reluctant as he was to give it to her, lest any evidence on it be destroyed, Martelli could not, under the circumstances, deny the woman what she obviously considered her daughter's most sacred possession. And truth be told, the NYPD had no right to withhold the diary from her, given no search warrant had been issued for the house in general and the bedroom in particular.

Martelli handed the diary to Mrs. Thompson, who clutched it to her chest and began sobbing. She moved toward Martelli so quickly that he had no choice but to put his arms around her and comfort her. A minute passed before she was able to compose herself, step back, and dab her eyes with a tissue.

"I'm sorry, Detectives. It's like I've received a message from the grave, a message from my daughter. I don't know how I *ever* will be able to repay you.

"I have no idea what I will find on the pages of this book, but whatever it is, I will know they are the most heartfelt thoughts of a wonderful, loving daughter."

She started to sob again, still clutching the diary tightly to her chest.

For one of the few times in his life, Martelli was not sure how to proceed. He and O'Keeffe needed to see the contents of the diary in the worst way, given it contained the last writings of the young woman who now appeared to be central to their investigation. On the other hand, they had no right to seize the book.

The men waited for Patricia Thompson to compose herself. Finally, Martelli spoke. "Mrs. Thompson, this is quite a revelation, and one I'm sure you'll want to share with your husband."

"Oh, no, I can't do that, at least not now. Emily's death was devastating to him. For months I heard him crying in the shower every morning after her death. Frankly, I feared he might take his own life. He was very fragile for almost a year afterwards, but fortunately, had the foresight and strength to seek professional help. I can't let him see this until I have read it. Depending on what I find, I may *never* be able to let him see it. But now, no . . . I'm afraid that won't be possible."

Martelli nodded. "I understand. And please know how difficult this is for me to say, but there may be things your daughter wrote that can help us piece together what may have happened to Trent Morrison. It's possible, for example, a friend confided in your daughter how angry he or she was and what they were going to do to one or more of those football players if they ever had the opportunity. We have no idea what we'll find, but I think we all want to know the truth. I think *Emily* would want us to know the truth."

Mrs. Thompson slowly nodded her head in agreement. "I understand what you are saying, Detective Martelli. What do you suggest? I really don't want to let this book out of my hands for very long, if that's possible."

Martelli knew it might be a day or two until they returned to Manhattan. He also knew the chances of finding fingerprints other than Emily's on the diary were small.

"What I'd like to propose is that while Detective O'Keeffe continues to go through Emily's room, I'll run into town, find a print and copy house, and make a digital copy of the diary for the Department's use. By the time I get back, Sean should have completed his work, you'll have the original copy of diary back, and we'll be on our way."

Patricia Thompson handed Martelli the book.

Twenty

While Martelli drove into town in search of a print and copy shop, O'Keeffe continued to search for evidence in Emily Thompson's room. One photograph on the wall over the young woman's desk in particular caught his attention. It was of three cheerleaders decked out in their uniforms and obviously taken at one of the school's games. The girls were all smiles and shaking their pom-poms for the photographer.

"Mrs. Thompson, who are these girls?"

O'Keeffe carefully removed the picture frame from the wall and handed it to the woman. She smiled. "Well, that's Emily in the middle. Isn't she beautiful?" Emily was a tall, statuesque brunette with long brown hair worn in a ponytail.

"The girl on her left is Joanne Baldwin. On her right is Kimberly Lathrope. The three of them were inseparable. If you saw one, you saw all three. They were like sisters. When Emily died, the other two quit the cheerleading team and other than going to classes, withdrew completely from school activities. It was devastating for them, as it was for us, and they, like us, grieved for many months. The girls even insisted on having an empty seat reserved between them for Emily, who was awarded a posthumous degree at graduation."

"May I take the photograph out of the frame and take a picture of it with my cell phone, Mrs. Thompson?"

"Of course, Detective."

O'Keeffe carefully removed the backing, and with the photograph lying flat on the desk, photographed and e-mailed a snapshot to Martelli, Dugan, and himself. Then he returned the picture to its frame and the frame to the wall.

"That should do it. Thanks."

O'Keeffe continued to search among Emily Thompson's belonging. Her clothes drawers revealed nothing other than what one might expect to find in a young woman's bedroom. O'Keeffe even looked under her bed, and much to his surprise, found a street sign, obviously taken as a prank by her and perhaps some friends in a modest show of defiance.

Mrs. Thompson shook her head and laughed. "Well, I guess she wasn't the perfect child after all, Detective. I hope this misdemeanor won't be held against her."

"I won't say anything if you won't," replied O'Keeffe, winking.

The search went on for another 45 minutes, but yielded nothing of evidentiary interest. By the time O'Keeffe had satisfied himself nothing more could be learned from what they had seen in the room, Martelli returned with the diary and a memory stick containing a PDF copy of its contents. The maid let him in and showed him to the second-floor bedroom.

"I've got the diary right here for you, Mrs. Thompson. Thanks so much for your help and understanding."

He handed the book to Patricia Thompson, who took it with both hands. "It is *I* who should thank *you*. If it wasn't for Detective O'Keeffe, we never would have found this treasure. I will forever be grateful you came here today."

■ *Theodore Jerome Cohen*

Twenty-one

'D id you receive Emily Thompson's diary, Missy?" Martelli was on his cell phone with the speakerphone on as he and O'Keeffe set off for lunch. "I sent it about an hour ago in PDF format from town. Thought you might have a few minutes later today to scan it for anything that might be of interest."

"Yeah, I got it. Went through it while having lunch. Poor thing. It's filled with the usual romantic fantasies, high drama, and bad choices many teenage girls write about. She sure had the hots for someone named Derek Hamilton, but he, apparently, never wanted to be anything more than a good friend."

"Where do Morrison, Hallaway, and Chapman fit into the picture?"

"Oh, they loom large in this legend, that's for sure. Morrison attempted to put the moves on her more than once, and he wasn't very gentlemanly about it. In fact, on one occasion, he cornered her in the basement of the field house and groped her."

Martelli looked angry. It appeared he was picturing the assault on Emily Thompson as one on his daughter. "Does it say what she did?"

"She managed to break away and run into the coach's office, but there's no indication she told anyone but the two girls who were her best friends."

"And they were . . .?"

"Joanne Baldwin and Kimberly Lathrope."

"Was that the only assault by Morrison on Emily?"

"Oh, no, there were several others. The man was a predator. Once, he groped her at an after-game party in a classmate's home. Another time, he grabbed her breast in a stairwell as they passed each other. The guy was a monster."

"What about Hallaway and Chapman?"

"They more or less acted as Morrison's lieutenants. If he said jump, they jumped. So, if Emily rebuffed Morrison and he gave the word, Hallaway and Chapman made her life miserable."

"How?"

"Based on what I read, they'd spread rumors about her throughout the school. Said things about how she slept around, what a slut she was, and the like."

"What about the entries following the rape? Those, obviously, would comprise the last several weeks' entries."

"Those are the most gut-wrenching, Lou. She wrote first about how she came home after the three boys raped her and stood in the shower for more than an hour, trying to wash their 'filth' off her body. By the way, they appeared to use condoms so as to avoid leaving evidence. At least she didn't have to worry about STDs. Then she goes through the entire scenario repeatedly, over and over again, day after day, for several days . . . how she told first Morrison, then Hallaway, and finally Chapman to get off her and stop. It appears Baldwin and Lathrope came into the room at some point and yelled at the boys, but they were thrown out."

"Who took the pictures?"

"It's not clear. In situations like that, it's usually more than one person, especially if they're taking turns assaulting a woman. Everybody wants a 'trophy shot.'"

"How did she get home?"

"From what she said, Baldwin and Lathrope enlisted Hamilton, who went into the room and talked the boys into releasing Emily. At that point, Baldwin and Lathrope got her dressed, and they and Hamilton drove her home. How she managed to hold it all together and not alarm her parents that night is beyond me."

"What happened next?"

"Well, by the next Monday, those pictures of the assault and rape were all over the school. Someone must have worked overtime in a darkroom over the weekend, that's for sure.

"Anyway, Morrison and his minions heaped ridicule and insults upon the poor girl to the point where she withdrew from classes for several days. Hamilton defended her honor, and for that he was beaten behind the school on Wednesday of that week. After another week passed, Emily finally told her parents what had happened. They immediately filed charges with the police on their daughter's behalf against the boys for assault, battery, and rape."

"And that's when the *real* problems began within the community," Martelli declared.

"Oh, yes. It was Emily's word against those of the three boys. And given who they were and where they stood in the school's pecking order *and the community's eyes*, it was no contest. Even many of the other girls on the cheerleading squad stood behind the three accused rapists."

Missy continued. "You can almost hear the desperation in her words as she writes her entries, day after day, the utter agony she endured when few outside her family and circle of close friends believed her story.

"You get the first hint she is contemplating suicide a few days before she actually kills herself when she says 'I don't know how much longer I can put up with this.' Oh, and there's this entry, on the morning she died. 'There's no hope. It's over.'

"I checked the date on that last entry, Lou. It's the day after the DA decided not to pursue the case against her three attackers."

Martelli shook his head. "That poor girl. She never stood a chance. If someone did that to my child, I honestly can say I don't know what I would do to them.

"Is there anything, *anything,* whatsoever in the diary to suggest someone she knew might seek to avenge her assault and rape?"

"Well, her two best friends actually carried out a guerilla war, of sorts, against the boys. There is mention of them letting the air out of the boys' car tires, breaking their car windows, and other acts of vandalism. But as to documented threats, no, I didn't see any."

"Missy, I have to ask this because it's been on our minds since Sean found the diary. What do you think the impact will be on Mrs. Thompson when she reads what her daughter wrote, and especially what Emily wrote in the last few days before she killed herself?"

"I knew you were going to ask me that, Lou. It was on my mind the entire time I was reading the diary. I almost felt the girl was speaking to me . . . that I could hear her voice crying out for help.

"It will rip your heart out toward the end. But I will tell you this, you can read through the depths of her despair and see the love she has for her mother and father as well as the appreciation she had for what they were attempting to do for her.

"And if you're worried about the message the Thompsons will take away from Emily's writings, don't. That piece I read to you earlier, 'There's no hope. It's over.' It wasn't the last entry in the diary."

"What was the last entry?"

"'I love you, Mommy and Daddy. I always will. Please don't blame yourselves for what I am about to do. I love you, Emily.'"

No one said anything for several seconds.

Finally, Martelli spoke. "Thanks, Missy. That makes Sean and me feel better.

"We're going to find a place for lunch, now, and then, drive to the Chapman's. It would be nice to talk with the Hallaways, but given the exhumation of their son's body took place only yesterday, it's probably best to let things settle down a bit.

"Oh, I almost forgot, if you have a chance, see if you can locate Joanne Baldwin and Kimberly Lathrope. According to the high school principal, Baldwin left the area after graduation and never returned. But he thought Lathrope was still living in upstate New York."

"Gee, Lou, anything else I can do for you while I keep the NYPD systems and software running in tip-top shape? Being an IT specialist really is only a part-time job for me, you know" she teased factiously, "so don't hold back. I live only to serve you and the First Precinct."

"This is why they pay you the big bucks, Dugan!"

The line went dead.

■ *Theodore Jerome Cohen*

Twenty-two

It was mid-afternoon before Martelli and O'Keeffe could reach Dan Chapman's parents by telephone. Andrew Chapman was at work, but Olivia, his wife, graciously agreed to meet with them. The men immediately drove over to the Chapman's residence.

The Chapman's lived to the west of Syracuse on a well-manicured plot of land adjoining an 18-hole golf course. All of the homes were built in the American colonial style, with stone and brick used extensively for their façades. Mrs. Chapman met the detectives at the door and invited them into the sitting room. The men handed her their cards.

"Please sit. May I offer you something to drink or eat?"

Martelli replied they had just come from eating lunch and were full.

"This isn't about the money the state owes my son, is it? That nice lady from the government said there was money waiting for my son in Albany. Just like the government to keep someone's money and not tell them about it. It's bad enough they tax us the way they do, but then, to keep our money and not even tell us? I tell you, I simply don't know what the world is coming to these days."

"No, ma'am, this isn't about your son's money. And I assure you, the money's safe. All he has to do is contact the Comptroller's Office. They'll be more than happy to send him the money."

"Oh, that's so wonderful to hear, Detective—" She looked at his card. "Martelli. Hmmm ... Italian, I see." And your partner is . . . Irish. You two remind me of the odd couple." She chuckled smugly.

Martelli grinned. "Well, we do have some interesting times together, that's for sure. But I'll tell you what, Mrs. Chapman, just to help your son out, if you can tell us the best way to reach him, I, personally, will make sure he has all the information and forms he needs to obtain his money in the shortest time possible."

"Why, Detective, that is *so* kind of you." She rose, walked to her desk, and took out a piece of personalized stationery. Using a fountain pen, she wrote her son's name, his address in Manhattan, and his home telephone and cell phone telephone numbers on the stationery. Then she waved the piece of paper in the air to ensure the ink dried quickly.

"Here you are. You shouldn't have any trouble finding him. However, he's out of the country right now . . . won't be back for several days, I'm told. But I'm sure he will be happy to hear from you."

Martelli took the piece of paper, folded it, and put it in his shirt pocket. "Thank you, Mrs. Chapman. I'll have everything ready for him by the time he returns. By the way, we understand he was an honor graduate of the Marquis de La Fayette High School. We've heard wonderful things about that institution."

"Oh, yes, one of the finest private high schools on the East Coast. My Danny was the salutatorian, you know. He finished with a 3.97 grade point average. If it hadn't been for that awful Mrs. Bartenelli—she gave him a B in English Literature, you know—he would have had straight A's and tied for valedictorian."

She turned away and stuck her nose in the air.

"Well, you certainly have much to be proud of, Mrs. Chapman. And look at what he's accomplished since leaving high school."

"Yes, he's been very successful, to say the least. He has two undergraduate degrees, one in Marketing and another in Finance. His employer is so impressed with him he's now paying for his studies leading to an MBA."

"So," chimed in O'Keeffe, "that unpleasant situation involving Emily Thompson never impacted him in the least."

Chapman's head snapped to the left. In an instant she was staring directly into O'Keeffe's eyes. If looks could kill, O'Keeffe, in that split second, would already have been dead and buried. "That slut!" she hissed. "What she put my son and his friends through was a travesty!

"Everyone knew she was sleeping around. My Danny's a good boy. He never would do anything like what she accused him of doing. He had a wonderful girlfriend at the time—Christine deGrace—and there was no need for him even to be associated with the likes of Emily Thompson, much less do what she and her parents accused my son of doing!"

O'Keeffe did not back off. "Well, there *was* conflicting evidence in the case, Mrs. Chapman. And things did get out of hand at that party, according to almost everyone present."

"Are you insinuating my son lied, Detective? For your information, the district attorney investigated the matter, and he came to the conclusion there was no case. No case, Detective O'Keeffe!" She pounded her fist on the coffee table to drive home the point.

"Now, I think you and Detective Martelli should leave. I'm finding this discussion distasteful."

She rose, and motioned them to the door.

Martelli and O'Keeffe bid her goodbye.

Twenty-three

"That went well, I think," Martelli laughed as they got into his car. "And look at all the things we learned. Like, I didn't know you were Irish. That's amazing."

"Aye, of the Irish clan called *O'Caoimb*. And talk about amazing, Lou . . . here we've worked together all this time, and I had to learn from someone else you're Italian. Scheesch, you think you know someone, and then they pull shit like that on you. I tell you, I simply don't know what the world is coming to these days."

Their *repartee* was interrupted by the distinctive ringtone on Martelli's cell phone associated with a call from Michael Antonetti—*Who Are You*, the theme from the television show <u>CSI</u>. Martelli grabbed his phone and touched the screen, enabling the call. "Yes, Michael. What's up?"

"The team from CSU finished about an hour ago. Unfortunately they found nothing inside the casket that will benefit your case. As well, I opened the viscera bag, which was tucked below Hallaway's shoes. Louis, his internal organs are in terrible shape. I doubt seriously we'll learn much from them when we run new tox screens."

"So, what you're telling me is that we've come up empty-handed."

"*Au contraire, mon bon ami.* I checked Hallaway's mouth, and *voilà*, there it was, another Charon's obol, very similar to the one we found in Morrison's mouth."

"I had a suspicion we'd find one, Michael. But you knew that all along, didn't you?"

Antonetti chuckled. "Of course. Besides, I read the Onondaga County medical examiner's report. He did a thorough job on the autopsy. I never thought a second autopsy would produce anything of value but had a hunch you had ulterior motives.

"The fact we found a coin, Louis, tells us Hallaway's demise, by whatever means, is linked to Morrison's. At the least, the possibility exists both were murdered."

"Absolutely. As for the Onondaga County medical examiner, there's always the possibility he initially missed the coin during the performance of the autopsy on Hallaway, just as we did with Morrison. But that's irrelevant. The fact is, the appearance of the coin is circumstantial evidence. It could have been put in Hallaway's mouth by the killer at the time Hallaway died or by a mourner when his body was open to the public for viewing in the funeral home or church where services were held.

"Look, Michael, for political reasons, we should ascribe its presence to the latter, and record it as fortuitous the county medical examiner had the foresight to call for a second autopsy."

114

"You're right. Let's make him look like someone who's on top of his game, able to anticipate the needs of an investigation such as ours, and come up with a plan of action to assist another jurisdiction involved in what may be a related case.

"You may as well be the one to break the news to him, Michael. And be sure to tell him we'll give him full credit for the assistance he provided to the NYPD when the case is finally cracked."

"I'll do that. Meanwhile, I'll get the coin over to Sergeant Reynolds at CSU and see if he can lift a print from it."

"Good. And when you're done taking whatever samples you need from Hallaway's organs, you might as well bundle him up and send him back to Onondaga County."

"I'll take care of it. What are your plans?"

"Sean and I have one more call to make . . . on the Hallaways. Then, we'll catch a good night's sleep and hit the road early tomorrow morning."

"Oh, Louis . . . one more thing."

"Yes?"

"I got the tox screens back on Morrison. There's no question someone slipped him a mickey, and a pretty strong one at that. We found significant quantities of chloral hydrate in his blood. The evidence is circumstantial, to be sure, but at this point, it's looking more and more like he was murdered."

Martelli thought for a moment. "Let's just keep that bit of information within the Department for the time being."

Twenty-four

M artelli and O'Keeffe were not able to meet with James and Allison Hallaway in their home south of Syracuse until late that evening.

The Hallaway's initially were reluctant to meet with the two detectives. This reluctance stemmed not only from the recent exhumation of their son's body, but also, because talking about their son would reopen old wounds that never had healed . . . their son's downward descent into a life of hell after returning from the Army and, ultimately, his death from what was believed to have been a drug overdose. The Hallaways relented, however, when Martelli explained how important it was for all parties to understand fully how their son had died.

James Hallaway met the detectives at the door and ushered them into the home's luxurious living room. Mr. Hallaway was a member of the boards of directors of several corporations, including one of the major US industrial corporations listed on the New York Stock Exchange. His wife also served on several boards, and they spent much of the year traveling throughout the US, attending board of director meetings.

The detectives handed their cards to Mr. Hallaway, who invited the men to sit. Meanwhile, Mrs. Hallaway went into the kitchen, returning moments later with coffee and sweets, which she set on the coffee table in front of them.

Mr. Hallaway began the conversation. "I'm sure you can understand our reluctance to meet with you this evening, Detectives. But when the medical examiner approached us about exhuming Brian's body and told us about how Trent Morrison had died under similar circumstances, we could hardly refuse."

Martelli nodded. "First, Mr. Hallaway, I want to express our Department's appreciation for your cooperation. You have been very helpful under the most difficult of circumstances. Second, yes, unfortunately, Mr. Morrison also died of an apparent heroin overdose compounded by an excessive intake of alcohol. That said, there still are some things that need, shall we say, *clarification* regarding the manner in which Mr. Morrison died."

Mrs. Hallaway look puzzled. "But I thought you said he died as a result of a heroin overdose, didn't you?"

"Yes, that's true. What we're not sure of is whether or not someone was with him at the time he died."

Mr. Hallaway knew instantly the implications of Martelli's statement. "So, you're saying, there's the possibility someone might be complicit in his death . . . that there's even a possibility he was murdered."

"No, I haven't said that. I'm merely stating the fact we have encountered evidence inconsistent with Mr. Morrison being alone at the time of his death. As such, we are required to resolve these inconsistencies. When we learned your son had died under similar circumstances, and given the former relationship between the two men, we were obligated to investigate your son's death as well."

The Hallaways nodded their understanding.

"Detectives, please don't be bashful. Help yourselves to coffee and Danish," Mrs. Hallaway prodded.

Martelli poured a cup of coffee for O'Keeffe and one for himself. Then, he selected a small cheese Danish and placed it on the dessert plate in front of him. "I'll have to spend two days in the gym when I get home, especially after eating a few of these. I'm sure they're delicious."

"Take as many as you like, Detective. I baked them myself."

Martelli took a bite, wiped his mouth with the small linen napkin at his place, and took out his notepad. "If you don't mind, I'd like to ask a few questions, some of which, given the circumstances, might make you a little uncomfortable. But please understand, anything you can tell us could be very important in clarifying events surrounding both your son's and Mr. Morrison's deaths."

James Hallaway nodded. "We understand, Detective."

"Obviously, one of the first questions we ask in a situation such as this is, was there anyone you know who might have wanted to harm your son?"

The Hallaways looked at each other and shook their heads 'no.'

James Hallaway shrugged. "I certainly can't think of anyone. Brian was always very popular in high school. He played football, you know—a wide receiver—the best the school ever had. Really made his mark there. He was one of three players nicknamed The Flying Horsemen who set record after record and who took the school to two successive division championships. Under Trent Morrison, there simply was no stopping them."

"And remember, dear, how well he did academically," his wife reminded him. "Our son was at one time in the upper ten-percent of his class. He excelled in science and math. Everyone thought he had a brilliant future in front of him as an engineer, and then . . . ." Her voice trailed off.

"And then?" asked Martelli.

"And then," she continued, "there was that dreadful lawsuit involving Emily Thompson. She accused our son, Trent Morrison, and Dan Chapman of raping her at a party following one of the games. Detectives, my son would *never* do that. He was taught to respect women. He was dating a wonderful girl from his class and, in fact, they were going steady. It was unthinkable he would even *think* about doing such a thing."

O'Keeffe brought up the subject of the pictures taken at the party. "Based on discussions with a number of sources, some of the photographs show everyone cited in the lawsuit with Emily Thompson in the bedroom where she claimed she was attacked and raped. Several shots show the boys, including your son, striking 'victory' poses over Thompson's body. And from the glazed look in their eyes, all of them, including Ms. Thompson, appear to have been drinking."

"My son didn't deny everyone was horsing around, Detective," Mrs. Hallaway asserted. "And yes, they never should have been drinking. But the district attorney did a thorough investigation into the matter, and he decided not to pursue the case. We believed our son and the other boys. In the end, they were exonerated."

Both Martelli and O'Keeffe were furiously taking notes. Martelli was the first to speak. "Did anyone ever threaten your son as a result of that incident?"

James Hallaway shrugged. "Threats? I don't know. Brian mentioned from time to time he'd come out of school and find the tires on his Corvette flat. He also mentioned someone had shattered Trent Morrison's car windows on one occasion. I have to believe those were, in part, the result of the failed lawsuit, but no one ever was caught and prosecuted. Some thought the vandalism was nothing more than teenage pranks."

The room was silent for a moment.

Then, Mr. Hallaway spoke. "But you recall, Allison, Brian never was the same after that."

Allison Hallaway slumped in her chair. "Yes," she said, her voice suddenly weak. "The light seemed to go out of his eyes. He just wasn't the same anymore. Oh, he still was able to play football. My god, could that boy play football. When he was with Trent and Dan on the field, he was alive.

"But he seemed to lose interest in everything else. He broke up with his girlfriend, his grades started slipping . . . he became a different person. He graduated, but not in the top ten percent of his class. And after a lackluster summer, most of which he didn't work, he went off to one of the top engineering colleges in the Midwest, quit mid-semester, and enlisted in the Army.

"When he separated from the Army several years later and returned home, it was clear something was wrong. He couldn't hold a job, always seemed angry, and simply made our lives miserable. It wasn't long before he began drinking and using drugs. Finally, we asked him to leave. It was the most painful decision of our lives. But he was destroying us as a family, and—"

Allison Hallaway began to weep. James Hallaway went to her, and gently put his arms around her shoulders. "I couldn't let him do that, Detectives. It was my decision that he leave. I don't regret it. It had to be done. I tried working with various social and veterans agencies in the area to get him help, but as you know, if the person you're trying to help doesn't want what's being offered, nothing you do can change the situation."

Martelli nodded. He leaned forward, took a sip of his coffee, finished his Danish, and after wiping his mouth with the napkin, settled back to ask another question. "When was the last time you spoke with your son, Mr. Hallaway?"

He thought for a moment. "Well, let me see . . . it was a week or so before he died. Yes, we got a call to come to the emergency room of the local hospital. This was the third time we had been called to the ER within a period of a few months, each time because Brian had been brought in after being found on the street, drunk or high on drugs. This time was by far the worse.

"When he recovered enough to talk, he seemed very apprehensive, almost as if he were afraid of something. He said he had seen someone he hadn't seen since high school. A woman, he said. He was very sure about that. He wondered why she was coming back into his life now and what she wanted. He said he wanted to confront her, but she hurried away."

Martelli leaned forward. "Did he happen to mention the woman's name or perhaps describe her? Maybe he mentioned the color of her hair or a class they might have taken together? Anything?"

"No. If he had said something specific, I'm sure it would have stuck in my mind."

O'Keeffe ate the last of his two pieces of Danish, touched the napkin to his lips, and picking up his notepad asked, "What happened to your son's belongings after he died?"

James Hallaway chuckled. "What belongings? When they brought him to the hospital, he had nothing but the clothes on his back. I'm sure by the time he returned to the street, whatever he may have left out there was already stolen from him by others in the same boat. If you're not out there to guard your belongings, Detectives, they'll be gone in a heartbeat. I gave him a couple hundred dollars for food and lodging, and that was the last time we saw him alive."

O'Keeffe nodded. "I was hoping he might have encountered the woman after his release and left something that would help us to identify her. But I guess that's out of the question."

Suddenly, James Hallaway appeared to remember something. "Wait, I do recall one thing my son said."

The Detectives' ears perked up.

"He was still a little groggy while we were talking, but I remember now. He said something like 'I wish Danny had never let Tia date Trent.'"

Martelli and O'Keeffe looked at each other.

"And that's it?" asked Martelli.

"That's it," replied James Hallaway. "I thought he might be talking about his former teammate, Dan Chapman. But I haven't a clue who Tia was or what the problem might have been. And frankly, I didn't think that was the time to press him for more information. The man was barely able to function on his own, much less carry on a rational conversation.

"I wish I could be more helpful."

"No, no, Mr. Hallaway," Martelli protested, "that comment may turn out to be very important. Thank you for telling us."

The room went silent. Finally, Martelli rose. "I think we're done for now. This has been most helpful. Detective O'Keeffe and I'll head back to our motel and let you get on with your evening."

Everyone rose, shook hands, and said goodbye. Once outside, the men got into Martelli's *Crown Vic* for the trip back to their motel.

■ *Theodore Jerome Cohen*

Twenty-five

"**I** have the strange feeling we're missing something important here," Martelli said as they pulled away from the Hallaway's residence.

"What?" responded O'Keeffe, rhetorically. "That Brian Hallaway's and Dan Chapman's worlds revolved around Trent Morrison's? That wouldn't be unusual. Morrison called all the shots on the field, and from the sound of it, he called the shots off the field as well."

"You're right, Sean. The quarterback is king, if not by position, then by decree. Just look at any high school prom and tally the number of quarterbacks who are elected to the position of prom king. They have their choice of girls, usually date the most attractive ones available—by the score—and have no compunction about taking a girl from a friend if the mood strikes."

"You want my opinion, Lou? I think Dan Chapman was dating a young woman named Tia for whom he cared very much. Morrison decided he wanted that woman and 'asked' Chapman if it would be all right to date her. Chapman didn't have a choice, of course. And the poor girl was fed to the wolves . . . or in this case, the wolf.

127

"In fact, I think something very bad happened on one or more dates with Morrison, something that possibly involved Brian Hallaway. Whatever anger that girl Tia had for The Flying Horsemen, then, was only heightened when—and this is just me talking—the three of them, in a drunken stupor, assaulted and raped Emily Thompson at that party, basically ignoring, if not seriously embarrassing, Chapman's former girlfriend and in no uncertain terms letting her know she no longer was worthy of their attention."

Martelli nodded in agreement. "That would be a hellava blow to someone's ego, all right. But it happens all the time in high school, though not quite so dramatically in most cases, I would hope. And even if that's what happened, why didn't the perp kill Hallaway and Morrison years ago? She apparently had no trouble finding them. Why now? What's the trigger? What event set everything in motion?"

"Good question. I certainly don't have the answer. And if this line of reasoning leads to the perp, then I'm not sure Joanne Baldwin and Kimberly Lathrope can be called persons of interest. After all, they may have been close friends of Emily Thompson, and they even may have been behind some of the vandalism reported after the lawsuit was dropped, but it hardly sounds as if they would have dated Morrison, Hallaway, or Chapman."

Twenty-six

'Come on, Lover Boy, we need to get on the road." It was a little past 6 AM the following morning when Martelli banged on O'Keeffe's motel door.

O'Keeffe answered the door, bath towel around his waist, cell phone to his ear. He held up his forefinger, signaling 'one minute' to Martelli, as O'Keeffe spoke with his fiancé, Susan Allerton, MD, whose practice was in Lake George, NY. "Okay, Sweetheart, give my love to Heather and tell her I'm coming to see you both very soon." He made a kissing sound into the mouthpiece and ended the call.

"And don't you dare say a word to anyone at the precinct about that kiss, Lou, or they'll never find your body, I promise you that!"

"What? What did I say?" responded Martelli, throwing his hands into the air.

"I know what was going through that mind of yours. And for God's sake, don't say anything to Dugan. She'll grab ahold of that, and I'll never hear the end of it!"

"Your secret is safe with me, Sean."

"By the way, Lou, remember the comment you made about what you would do if anyone did something to your daughter. You know, if they did anything like what those boys did to Emily Thompson?"

"Yeah. But as I recall, I said I honestly didn't know *what* I would do to them."

"Well, I've been giving it a lot of thought. Heather, Susan's daughter, is 12 years old. It won't be long before she's a teenager and some jerk with red-hot gonads shows up at the door—assuming he even deigns to get out of his car and come to the door—to pick her up for a date. So, I'm thinking. Fear is good. A lot of fear—I mean the kind of stuff that makes a guy lose his water—may be the best way to head problems off at the pass."

"I don't like where this conversation is heading."

"No, no, Lou, listen, you're really going to love this." O'Keeffe seemed quite taken with an idea he had concocted. "You might even want to try this if you have trouble with any of Tiffany's boyfriends."

Martelli rolled his eyes. "Okay, I know your itching to tell me, so what is it?"

"So, this is what I'm going to do," O'Keeffe continued. "When Heather's date comes to the door, I'm gonna greet him wearing a black shoulder holster containing my Smith and Wesson *Model 29* revolver."

Martelli started laughing. "Well, that would scare the shit out of me, all right. You and Dirty Harry. You're gonna need to keep toilet paper by the door if you pull a stunt like that."

Martelli could not believe what he was hearing. Laughing deeply, tears started rolling down his cheeks.

O'Keeffe started laughing, too. "Okay, okay, get this. I even know what I'm gonna say to the poor guy. 'Hi, I'm Heather's dad.' You know I'm gonna adopt her, Lou. 'Meet my friends, Smith and Wesson. They said you're to treat Heather real nice and have her back no later than ten o'clock. Otherwise, the three of us are gonna come looking for you. Booyah!'

"Waddaya think, Lou?"

Martelli took out his handkerchief and still laughing, started to dry his eyes. "I think Susan and Heather will take your beloved Smith and Wesson revolver and use it to put *you* out of *their* misery, that's what I think.

"Now, throw on a suit and tie so we can get breakfast and head back to New York."

————◦————

While they were waiting for their breakfast at a local diner, Martelli placed a call to Dugan. "Hey, good morning. And how is your day going?"

"Well, up until a few seconds ago, it was terrific. But then I got this call from some pain in the ass defective . . . ah, *detective* in upstate New York, and everything went into the shitter."

131

Dugan loved to play with the English language. If she could turn a phrase at someone else's expense, so much the better. "How's your day been?"

"Just peachy. Listen, you know those two women I asked you to check out?"

"You mean Joanne Baldwin and Kimberly Lathrope?"

"Yeah. I was thinking—"

"You're barking up the wrong tree, Lou, if you think they had anything to do with Morrison's and Hallaway's deaths."

"I had a feeling that might be the case, but how did you come to that conclusion?"

"Easy. I simply tracked them down, and with a little poking around, determined they couldn't possibly have murdered either vic."

"So, what did you learn?"

"Well, let's start with Joanne Baldwin. I was able to locate her family, which still has a home in the Syracuse area. The high school principal was correct. She did leave the area after graduation. In fact, she moved to Alaska, found work, and married. Unfortunately, she was stricken with multiple sclerosis about five years ago and is confined to a wheelchair. There is no way she could have committed those murders. She can't even walk without assistance."

"And Lathrope?"

"She's still in Syracuse . . . runs a stationery shop called Scribbles with an old high school friend. In fact, they are partners. I went to their Website and found a ton of pictures taken at an open house they had held in the shop on the night Morrison was killed. There are pictures showing Lathrope and her partner together with their clients discussing products, drinking wine and eating *hors d'oeuvres*, sharing a good joke, and the like. Unless they've repealed the Laws of Nature, there's no way she could have hosted that open house and killed Morrison at the same time."

"I had a feeling those two leads were going to take us nowhere. I'm sure it wouldn't even pay to check on what Lathrope was doing the night Hallaway died."

"I did . . . she and her partner were on vacation in the Caribbean. They posted date-time-stamped photos of their trip on the shop's Website."

"Well, that leaves us with only one lead."

"What's that, Lou?"

"On Hallaway's last trip to the ER, he said . . . what was that he said, Sean?" Martelli handed O'Keeffe his cell phone.

"Hi, Missy. Hallaway told his father, 'I wish Danny had never let Tia date Trent.'"

"Who's Tia?"

"We haven't a clue. Nor did the father. From the sound of it, she would appear to have been a classmate of the three men, but now you know everything we know."

Martelli turned to O'Keeffe. "Sean, let me talk to her for a minute."

O'Keeffe handed Martelli his phone.

"Missy, see if you can obtain a copy of the Marquis de La Fayette High School yearbook for the class in which The Flying Horsemen graduated. Once you have it, find a woman named Tia and track her down. I'll bet she has one hellava story to tell us."

"This will be easy!"

Martelli could almost hear Dugan rubbing her hands together. "Hey! I want you to do this without hacking into the high school's server or performing some other nefarious feats of digital legerdemain. Keep it nice and legal. I really do worry about the things you pull at times."

"Oh, that's great, just fucking great. This from the man who once told me, 'Stick with me, darlin', you'll either be farting through silk or sitting in Leavenworth.'"

"Well, you know what I mean. So, how are you going to get the yearbook?"

"Gee, Martelli, it's not like we're deriving Einstein's Special Theory of Relativity. There are plenty of Websites that make high school yearbooks available to alumni. My dad's mother, for example, attended West Division High School in Milwaukee during the mid-1920s. He wanted the picture of her taken for her classes' yearbook. So, he signed in *as her* on a Website hosting West Division's yearbooks, found the picture of his mother, and grabbed a screenshot. It wasn't rocket science."

"Pretty sharp, your Dad."

"Oh, yeah. The only problem was, he started getting e-mail addressed to his mother, announcing special offers from the Website administrator, which was fine except the woman, God rest her soul, would be 105 years old today."

Martelli laughed. "So, what name are you going to use when you sign in to access the Marquis de La Fayette High School yearbook?"

"Emily Thompson."

■ *Theodore Jerome Cohen*

Twenty-seven

Martelli and O'Keeffe had been on the road for two hours when Martelli's phone rang. "That didn't take long, Missy."

"Lou, I downloaded the entire yearbook for the class in which The Flying Horsemen graduated. There isn't anyone in the class named Tia. After I went through the individual class photos, I went back and not only went through all of the group photos, but also, read every last word in the text. Zilch. Zip. Nada! You and your partner, sir, are SOL."

"Dammit! I thought for sure that comment about Tia would yield a fresh lead. These cases could not be more confounding.

"Okay, thanks, Missy. We're going to have to put our heads together here and see if we can sort some things out. Have a great day."

"Bye, Lou. Drive safely."

Martelli pressed his foot on the accelerator and the *Crown Vic* leaped forward in response to his demand for speed. Their trip had been productive, but it was time to put the information they had gleaned from their interviews to work on solving what now was becoming more than a hunch. The circumstances surrounding the deaths of Morrison and Hallaway increasingly suggested both men had been murdered, with the crimes committed by the same cold-blooded killer. Further, it appeared the men knew their killer, a woman. But what had been or was her relationship with them? These and other questions tormented Martelli and O'Keeffe, who also were struggling with the need to warn Dan Chapman his life could be in imminent danger.

Twenty-eight

'**A**dam, it's Lou Martelli." It had been a while since Deputy Coroner Antonetti had sent the Charon's obol found in Brian Hallaway's corpse to NYPD's CSU, and this seemed as good a time as any to check on the evidence. "Were you able to lift a print from the coin?"

"Sorry, Lou," replied CSU Sergeant Adam Reynolds. "Same problem as last time . . . not even the hint of a fingerprint. The coin's surface is rough, and given the circumstances under which it was found, even if a print had originally been deposited, I doubt it would have survived in the corpse's mouth for as long as the body was in the ground."

Martelli looked dejected. "Man, we just can't catch a break on these cases. And truth be told, other than Antonetti's observation the tie-off on Morrison's arm was incorrectly positioned, his tox screen showed high levels of chloral hydrate, and a coin was found in his mouth, we have nothing substantial to take to the DA should we come up with a person of interest. *Nothing!* Who can say whether or not he injected himself? And even if someone was with him when he died and they put a coin in his mouth as part of some ancient ritual, there's no law against that.

"I understand, Lou. I'm sorry we weren't able to do more for you. And believe me, we don't feel great about letting you down. We're all in this together."

"Thanks, Adam. I know you and your team are the best in the business."

"Let me know if there's anything else we can do to help."

"I will. Say 'hi' to your bride."

"Same from here."

Martelli ended the call and dialed his wife. "How're doin', Baby? How're the kids?"

Martelli knew his wife wouldn't have long to talk, given the demanding responsibilities of her job at the HVAC shop she managed. But he hadn't spoken to her since the previous evening, and with the investigations of the two murder cases going poorly, he just wanted to hear her voice.

"We're doin' well, Lou. But I can tell from the sound of your voice that things may not be going all that well on your end. What's the problem?"

"Oh, one of the last leads we had on what we believe was a murder in Syracuse just came a cropper, so now, we're batting zero for two. Sean and I have one last lead in our hip pocket, and our first try to run *that* one to ground just failed. We just can't catch a break."

"That must be so frustrating. Out of curiosity, what's the lead?"

"One of the vics, just before he died, mentioned a woman named Tia. We assumed she was a high school classmate, but when Missy went through the yearbook for the appropriate year, she couldn't find anyone by that name."

"I'm not surprised, Lou. That's probably a nickname. We have a gal who works in the backroom doing accounting. We call her Tia. Her given name is Celestia. Have Missy run through the yearbook again and look for that name. If you still can't find it, I'd call the school."

Martelli was ecstatic. "Wow, you not only are the most beautiful woman in the world, you also are the most intelligent. How did I ever end up marrying you?"

"I guess you chased me until I caught you, Lou! See you for dinner?"

"I wouldn't miss it. Might even bring Sean along, so set another place at the table."

"Done! Drive safely. Love ya!"

Martelli was so excited he almost dropped his cell phone. In a flash he dialed Dugan, barely able to contain himself while the call went through.

"Scheesch, Martelli, can't I even get a moment's peace?"

"Missy, Steph broke the code. Tia is short for Celestia. Could you do another scan of the yearbook for that name and get back to me as quickly as possible? This may be the break we're waiting for."

"I'll do it right now, Lou."

He ended the call, revealing his excitement at the prospect of finally having a solid lead by adding ten miles per hour to the speedometer.

Twenty-nine

'We struck out, Lou." Barely 20 minutes had passed when Dugan was back on the phone with Martelli. "I did a quick scan of all the class photos, group photos, and text, just as you asked. I found nothing. If this lady attended school with those three men, she must have left prior to graduation.

"Your best bet, and perhaps your only option at this point, is to call the principal and see if he remembers anyone by the name of Celestia. It's such an unusual name that if she had been a student in his school, he'll probably remember her."

Martelli was despondent. He and O'Keeffe had been stymied by many a homicide in the past. But solving the Morrison and Hallaway murders—if that's what they were, and there was no question, at least in their minds, another party was involved in both men's deaths—presented them with virtually insurmountable obstacles. Every lead thus far had led to a dead end. And what remained was, at best, circumstantial evidence of someone who either witnessed the deaths or found the bodies soon after the men died . . . someone who, in both cases, and for some unknown reason, left an ancient coin under their tongues. *'That'll go over really big in the DA's office,'* Martelli thought to himself, *'O'Keeffe and I will be laughed off the Force.'*

143

"You're right, Missy. We don't have a choice at this point. I'll give him a call. Thanks for the quick turnaround. I'll get back to you if we learn anything."

"Yell if you need something, Lou. I want to help you guys."

Martelli ended the call, checked his phone for Ed Lane's telephone, and redialed the principal's number.

"Mr. Lane's office, Dorothy speaking."

"Dorothy, this is Detective Martelli. I wonder if Ed is available to talk with me for a few minutes."

"Good morning, Detective. I'm sorry, but Ed is speaking to a group in the auditorium at the moment. I expect he'll be available in about 15 minutes. Is there something I can help you with?"

"That's very kind of you, Dorothy, but I think I'd better talk directly with him. It's rather sensitive." He gave her his cell phone number and asked that he call as soon as he returned to the office.

It was almost 20 minutes before Martelli's cell phone rang. "Detective Martelli, this is Ed Lane. Dorothy said you had called about something she said was sensitive. I apologize for not being available when you called earlier."

"Not a problem, Ed. In going through some of the evidence we've collected, we stumbled on the name of someone we believe may have attended your school around the time

Morrison, Hallaway, and Chapman were students. Does the name Tia or Celestia ring a bell?"

"Oh, yes, of course. Celestia Hughes. Very bright young lady. Attractive, too. As I recall, she was here under a scholarship provided by an anonymous benefactor. Unfortunately, Tia left in the middle of her junior year. I must say, it was quite unexpected."

"How so?"

"Well, one day her father just walked into my office and abruptly pulled her out of school . . . said something about his being transferred out-of-country. The family was gone two days later, lock, stock, and barrel. No one ever saw them again. Nor did anyone ever learn what happened to her or her family. They simply vanished into thin air."

"Who did the father work for?"

"I haven't a clue . . . and before you ask, no, our records wouldn't show that kind of information. Yes, they would show a student's emergency contact names and telephone numbers, but in almost all cases, these would almost always be their parent's names and home telephone or cell phone numbers.

"I recall her mother was a stay-at-home mom because there were two much younger children in the family. We talked about them briefly on one parent-teacher's night at the high school."

Martelli thought for a moment. "Ed, when I was in high school, we had a photography club. Do you have one?"

"You bet, one of the best in the area."

"So, there were always lots of guys and gals taking photographs of just about anything and everything throughout the school year, and maybe into the summer?"

"Absolutely. In fact, we used to do most of our own film developing and printing using the old dark room in the basement of the administration building. Posted many of the club's photos on the bulletin boards throughout the school. Still do, in fact, though today everything is digital. We also use these photos in the school newspaper, for event publicity offsite—for example, on the bulletin boards at the local grocery and drug stores—and in our yearbooks."

"So it's safe to assume Tia appears in some of these photos, whether on purpose or by accident."

"I would think so, Detective."

"Ed, this is very important. You may be one of the few people who not only remember Tia, but also, who remember what she looks like.

"I know this may be an imposition, but could I ask you, for starters, to go through the school newspapers and photos for the years in which Tia was a student. If you find any pictures of her, any pictures at all regardless of their size and quality, please make copies using your cell phone and e-mail them to me. It's vital we find this woman.

"I wish I could tell you more. Perhaps someday I'll be in a position to do that. But for now, trust me when I tell you she may hold the key to our understanding of what happened to Trent Morrison and Brent Hallaway."

Lane didn't immediately respond. In fact, for a moment, Martelli thought he had lost the connection.

"Ed? Ed? Are you still there?"

"Yes, I'm still here, Detective. I don't know if I can do what you ask. Don't you need some kind of warrant to obtain those pictures? I mean, first of all, the pictures are of minors. And second, the photos are the property of a private institution—this high school."

"I understand your concerns, Ed. But as you said, many of the pictures are already in the public domain, so to speak, by having been published in the school newspaper, which certainly must have been taken outside the school, or by having been posted in stores around the local neighborhood.

"Now, we could get a judge to issue a warrant, if that's required. But frankly, if the press got wind of that, think what might happen when they start poking around. You certainly don't need the publicity, let alone the interruptions. And believe me, the press can be relentless . . . and ruthless. If there's even the whiff—"

"I get it, Detective. I'll do as you ask and be in contact as soon as I have something."

"And Ed—"

"Yes?"

"I don't have to tell you how sensitive this is. So please keep this just between us."

"I understand. You can count on me. I'll start looking through the school's newspapers and other photos as soon as we hang up."

Thirty

S ean sat silently through the entire exchange between Martelli and Ed Lane. He could hear both sides of the conversation. When his partner finally ended the call and put his cell phone on the seat next to him, O'Keeffe turned to him and chuckled. "I got news for you, Buddy. You don't stand a snowball's chance in Hell of finding that woman. I don't care if Ed gives you a thousand pictures of her—they could even have been taken yesterday—she'll never be found."

"What the hell are you talking about, Sean?"

"She's in the witness protection program, Lou."

"What?"

"Listen, no one goes from leading a fully integrated normal life, such as the Hughes did back in the mid-1990s, to disappearing without a trace within the span of two days unless they have massive amounts of help, the kind of help provided by the US government. And now, we just learned Celestia Hughes was attending that prestigious private school under a scholarship provided by an anonymous benefactor . . . as in *the US government.*

"Hellooooo. Wake up, Lou. Hughes wasn't even their real name. I don't know who in the family was being threatened— probably either Tia's father or mother, or both, and who knows what they may have seen or done to need protection— but the whole family was hiding in plain sight, and the Family Hughes was their cover. God only knows where they went and what new identities they were given when they were pulled out of Syracuse. But I'll say this, the Hughes sure appeared to have cut one sweet deal with the feds. Whatever happened to them in Syracuse sure must've turned their world upside down again."

The United States Federal Witness Protection Program, which sometimes is referred to as the Witness Security Program, or WITSEC, is administered by the US Department of Justice. The US Marshals Service is responsible for operating the service, which is designed to protect witnesses who have been threatened before, during, or after a trial. Those threatened and their families are moved to safe locations and given new identities with authentic documentation. Housing subsistence, living expenses, and medical expenses also are provided. There has *never* been a breach of security in which someone in the program or a family member has been harmed.

If Martelli had just begun to feel good about the latest turn of events, his partner's latest revelations instantly soured the day. "Well shit, O'Keeffe, aren't you one to throw a turd into the punch bowl!"

"Sorry to spoil the party, Lou, but them's the facts. And it's even more complicated than that. We don't even know if the Hughes, or whatever the hell their name is, are in the federal program or in one of the programs run by California, Illinois, New York, Texas, or any of the other states that run programs covering crimes not addressed by the federal witness protection program."

"Well, I can't tell you how great all this makes me feel," Martelli said factiously. "I don't even want to contemplate talking to the DOJ about the family, much less approach the Department on the subject. That sounds like a nonstarter from the get-go. And while I know we got away with breaking into the FBI's server in Quantico last year to obtain Bishop's correspondence and e-mails, I wouldn't dare ask Dugan to hack into the WITSEC server. Talk about getting the Blue Screen of Death!"

O'Keeffe shook his head. "So, is that the ballgame? Three strikes and we're out?"

Martelli furrowed his brows. His eyes were directed up into the right side of his brain. Suddenly, he appeared to have an idea. Snatching his cell phone, he deftly dialed Dugan.

"Missy, I need to ask you a question."

"The answer is, I have no idea why we never see baby pigeons, Lou."

"Funny. You have software that can age the picture of a person artificially, right?"

"I don't have it on my machine, but it's easy enough to obtain. I can call some friends in forensics at the FBI.

"The programs are known as virtual face-aging software. They're used to help find missing persons."

"Do they do a good job?"

"It depends on what you have to work with. It helps to have information on the person's personal history, family traits, and the like, but that's not absolutely necessary. The software incorporates large samples of faces and the way they have aged to calculate the *average* transformations expected over time. Why do you ask?"

"I turns out that Tia's family most likely was in either a state or federal witness security program. Chances of finding her are slim. But I've got the principal at her old high school digging up some pictures of her. If he can find some, I'm hoping you can develop a composite photograph of the girl and 'age' her so that we can put out a BOLO."

"Wow, you really are stretching things, Lou. But what you ask is certainly doable. Get as many pictures of the girl as you can. I'll digitally combine them to create a super-detailed composite. That'll give us the best chance of success once we invoke the face-aging software."

"I knew I could count on you, Missy. By the way, I didn't know you still had any friends over at the Bureau after that hacking caper last year."

Dugan laughed manically. "Oh Hell, Lou, the IT guys in Quantico and I are always helping each other out."

Thirty-one

The time was 8:30 PM. Martelli finally had made it home to Brooklyn after a long day on the road followed by several hours in the office going over what little evidence he and O'Keeffe had accumulated on the deaths of Morrison and Hallaway. With Morrison's death now appearing more and more to be a homicide, pressure had increased significantly to close the case. In addition, there still was the matter of Hallaway's death. Could it, too, have been murder? Martelli and O'Keeffe had virtually nothing in the way of evidence to answer that question definitively.

Martelli took off his suitcoat and draped it over a chair in the living room. Walking into the kitchen where Stephanie was reheating his dinner, he was struck by how quiet the house was. Normally he could hear the blaring of the television set or the sound of Tiffany and Rob arguing about one thing or another, as siblings are wont to do. But tonight, a strange quietness had settled over the Martelli household, and Stephanie's reticence seemed to give him a feeling of apprehension.

"What's going on, Steph? Where are the kids? It's too quiet."

His wife took his turkey dinner out of the oven and after setting the white meat, potatoes, and peas on a plate and adding cranberry sauce and a small salad, she set his dinner in front of him.

"Tiffany didn't have a good day, Lou. I've asked Rob to keep it down for a while so she can rest."

Martelli was alarmed. "Is she all right? Did something happen to her at school?"

"No, no, she's fine. But something must have happened at Mrs. Rodriguez's when she was over there after school, helping with her foster children. She came home shaking. When we hugged, she burst into tears. Oh, Lou, she just sobbed and sobbed. She almost couldn't catch her breath at times. I held her close, helped her climb the stairs, and got her into bed. It took a while, but I finally got her to fall asleep.

"I still don't know what the problem is. She kept saying she was all right, that there was nothing physically wrong with her, but she either couldn't or wouldn't tell me what happened."

Martelli scratched his head. From what Stephanie was saying, it appeared something traumatic had occurred, but what could it have been?

There were certain facts both he and his wife knew with certainty. Twice a week after school Tiffany volunteered to help Mrs. Rodriguez, who lived several blocks from the Martelli's home, take care of her foster children. The middle-aged woman sorely needed Tiffany's assistance. Three weeks earlier the borough had asked Mrs. Rodriguez to take on a third child—a six-year-old girl name Brianna—which placed an additional burden on a caregiver who already was acting as the foster parent for twin four-year-old boys.

Tiffany had always come home from Mrs. Rodriguez's bursting with stories about how cute the children were and how much they loved her and she, them. More often than not, her backpack was laden with drawings or artifacts the children had made for her using playdough or Popsicle sticks. Her room was full of these mementos, some gifts from earlier foster children who had either moved back with their mothers or on to other foster parents, or from the foster children currently residing with Mrs. Rodriguez. Today, however, something had changed.

Martelli, who had yet to take a bite, put down his fork, placed his napkin on the table, and standing, walked toward the stairs. "Maybe I should ask if she wants to talk to me," he said quietly.

Stephanie nodded. "This may be one of those times when a daughter needs her father's shoulder."

Martelli made his way slowly up the stairs and to his daughter's bedroom door, where he stood for a minute, listening. Not hearing anything, he knocked gently. A tiny voice responded from within.

"Who is it?"

"It's me, Honey. May I come in?"

"If you want to."

Martelli opened the door. The room was dark, with only the light from the hallway illuminating his daughter's bedroom. He saw her under the sheets, clutching her pillow. Even in the dim light he could see from the puffiness around her eyes she had been crying. When she saw him, she sat up, burst into tears, and threw her arms up, waiting for him to hug her.

He quickly walked to her bed, sat down, and embraced his daughter, smoothing her hair and kissing her forehead. Neither said a word for a minute, though if you were to ask them later, they would tell you it seemed much longer.

Finally, Martelli spoke. "I don't know what happened to upset you so, but anytime you want to talk about it, I'll be here to listen. No matter what it is, you know you can always talk to your mother and me. There's nothing—*nothing*—we can't talk about or work through together. We're family. Hell—and don't tell your mother I said that—"

Tiffany giggled. She knew if she did, her dad would have to 'donate' $5 to the Swearing Jar.

". . . If you guys can put up with your mother and me, you can put up with just about anything!" he said.

She giggled again. Taking a tissue from her nightstand, she dabbed her eyes and appeared to brighten some.

Martelli took her face gently in his hands, and looking into her eyes, smiled and asked, "So, do you want to talk, or would you rather rest a little more?"

"No, I think I want to talk," she said, tearing up. "But it won't be easy." She started to cry again and then caught herself, nodded, and calmed down.

"Why don't you tell me what happened today, just as if you were talking to your best friend at school."

Tiffany nodded. "Well, after school let out, I went over to Mrs. Rodriguez's like I always do. The twins had colds, so she really had her hands full. She asked me if I would spend some time with Brianna. She's the new little girl the agency placed with Mrs. Rodriguez three weeks ago. Oh, Daddy, her name is Brianna, and she's so beautiful. But she's always sullen and withdrawn. She never talks."

"Never?"

"Never. I never once heard her say a word. Whenever I've gone to help Mrs. Rodriguez, I find her sitting on a small chair in the corner of the living room, watching TV."

"Okay, so what happened today?"

"Well, I came in and there she was. She was watching a movie about motorcycle gangs. I'm sure Mrs. Rodriguez would not have put that on for her, so I'm guessing Brianna must have been playing with the remote control.

"Anyway, as I came into the room, Brianna pointed to the TV and said, 'That's the man who hurt me.' I turned around to see a really mean-looking man with a mustache and ponytail, wearing a bandana, and leering from the screen."

"What did you do then?" Martelli asked.

"Well, I sat down in front of her and drew her into my lap. I asked, 'Are you sure? That's just a movie. It's not real, you know.' And she said, 'Oh, no, I'm sure. That's the man who hurt me . . . he always hurts me. And sometimes, when he's angry, he hurts my mother, too.'"

Martelli nodded. "I assume you changed the channel."

"Oh, yes. In fact, I shut the set off and took her by the hand to the play table to make some things with playdough. It was the first time I was able to get her to do that. She even talked a little more, mostly about her mom and when she was going to see her again."

"Go on, Honey."

"Well, after Mrs. Rodriguez gave the boys some cold medicine and settled them down for a nap, she gave Brianna a snack. That's when I told her what had happened . . . you know, about the man on the TV screen and what Brianna had said.

"Mrs. Rodriguez pulled me to one corner of the kitchen and told me Brianna's mother's boyfriend had been molesting Brianna since the child was three years old. It was only by the grace of God that a neighbor had called police one night because of the noise in the mother's apartment. That's when Child Welfare Services was alerted to the abuse and took Brianna into their system.

"Oh, Daddy, how can *anyone* be so cruel to a child? What is wrong with this world?"

Martelli shook his head, reached out, and hugged his daughter tightly. He had no answers.

■ *Theodore Jerome Cohen*

<u>Thirty-two</u>

‘**I'm** sorry it's taken so long, Detective Martelli, but constant interruptions seem to be the story of my life." It wasn't until the middle of the next day before Martelli heard these words on a telephone call from Edward Lane, the high school principal.

"Tell me about it, Ed. So, what were you able to find?"

"I think you'll be pleased. But I wanted to talk to you before sending the material I found your way."

"I'm all ears."

"Well, I found seven photographs taken in Tia's sophomore and early junior years that should help you. Two were taken when she was rehearsing with the cheerleading squad, another shows her with Dan Chapman, of all people, and the others show her with various other classmates, including one apparently taken at a party showing her with Brent Morrison. That's the last one I could find. She left school a month after it was taken.

"It's pretty clear she was involved with The Flying Horsemen, which, frankly, surprises me. I never have thought she would associate with that crowd. But then, her being on the cheerleading squad and all, I guess it makes sense they eventually would pull her into orbit around them."

"Can you send those photos down here via e-mail, Ed?"

"Certainly, I'd be happy to do that. I just finished taking high-res shots of them using my cell phone and will ship the JPEGs to you, one by one. Just give me the e-mail address I should us."

Martelli gave the principal his office e-mail address.

"I'd also be happy to ship you hardcopies of the photographs, if the copies I'm sending aren't up to snuff."

"That's very generous of you, Ed. Let's see what my tech can do with your copies, and I'll let you know if we need the originals. I can't thank you enough for your help. Those photographs may be the break we need."

Thirty-three

It took but a minute before Martelli saw the first of seven e-mails from Ed Lane arrive in his Inbox. As each was received, he immediately forwarded it to both O'Keeffe and Dugan, alerting the latter by telephone to their availability as well.

"They should be coming in now, Missy. Work your magic. This is going to make or break the case, that's for sure."

"Nothing like a little pressure to make a gal feel wanted, Lou. For the life of me, I don't know how Stephanie puts up with you. It continues to amaze me why you haven't shown up buried in a shallow grave somewhere in Southern New Jersey by now!"

"You just don't understand the masculine mystique of us Martelli men, darlin'."

"Oh, I understand it all right. That's why I'm wearing my hip waders as we speak."

■ *Theodore Jerome Cohen*

Thirty-four

In the IT Lab, Dugan was busy developing a composite image of Celestia Hughes, or whatever her name was, using segments of the seven photographs provided by Hughes's former high school principal. Not all of the photographs were of the same quality. Nor did they show the subject from the same angle. But using her sophisticated photo processing software, Dugan was able to construct a full-face rendition of Hughes within two hours of receiving the raw material. She sent a copy of the product to both Martelli and O'Keeffe. When she was sure they had received it, she initiated a conference call with them.

"Okay, guys, you see what I've been able to do. Compare what I've done, if you would, with each of the seven photographs provided by the high school principal and tell me what you like or don't like."

Martelli was the first to speak. "Wow, this is incredible. You even captured the little scar on the left side of her chin."

O'Keeffe was equally impressed. "And the dimples in her cheeks. But I do note one thing, Missy."

"What's that, Sean?"

"On some of the photos, her beauty mark appears more prominent. Maybe she's using makeup or something. I don't know. What do you think about darkening it a bit in the composite?"

"Not a problem. Stand by."

The men could hear Dugan tapping furiously on her keyboard. In a few seconds, the bells on their computers rang, signaling the receipt of another e-mail from her.

"Take a look at this, Guys."

"Perfect," replied O'Keeffe.

"I'm going ahead with the BOLO, Missy. You done good, lady! Take the rest of the afternoon off with pay!"

"Gosh, Martelli, that's so thoughtful of you. I'll be sure to tell my boss how generous you are with his money."

Thirty-five

Martelli and O'Keeffe spent the next day catching up on their paperwork and waiting—*hoping*—for a response to the BOLO that had issued for Celestia Hughes. But nothing came in despite the woman's artificially aged image having been broadcast to federal, state, and local law enforcement agencies across the US.

On the following day, just after they had come to work at 7:30 AM, Martelli and O'Keeffe received an e-mail from Dugan with a Subject line 'Do You Recognize This Woman?'

Martelli opened the e-mail and the JPEG attachment. He did a double-take. Staring back at him was a woman who appeared to be Celestia Hughes. At the least, she was a dead ringer for the woman in the composite photograph created by Dugan. The problem Martelli could see was, according to Dugan's e-mail, the woman's name was Mackenzie Pierce, PhD. Importantly, she was a forensic archeologist with the National Archives for Ancient Cultures in Washington, DC.

Martelli yelled down the hall for O'Keeffe to come to his office. Once his partner arrived, they telephoned Dugan.

167

Martelli could barely contain himself. "How in the hell did you find her?"

Dugan laughed. "You guys are so incontinent . . . I mean *incompetent*.

"All you ever do is ask questions, put out BOLOs, and expect others to do the heavy lifting. So of course it's up to me to pull your fat out of the fire. But do I ever get the credit for my hard work? Oh, no. Does Commissioner Fields ever ask me to stand next to him at a major press conference like he does a certain detective-investigator I know? Of course not." At this point she turned the pathos up another notch. "It's just little ole me, working alone in the basement of 1PP, solving all the city's major homicides in my spare time."

Martelli didn't miss a beat. "Jesus, Missy, you don't have to bust our balls. Can't you just once present your findings without being such a drama queen?"

"Now what fun would that be, Lou? Besides, it would take all the mystery out of these little surprises I present you with." Here she went into her sing-song voice. "Anyway, you still haven't asked me the question. I'm waiting."

There was silence on the line. Finally, O'Keeffe pretended he couldn't take the suspense any longer. "Okay, okay, I give up," he cried in mock anguish. "How did you find her . . . or at least someone who stands a good chance of being the person we're looking for? We need to know so we can confirm your sources."

"Why, Sean, I thought you'd never ask.

"It was simple, actually. My little dog Chauncey woke me around 5 AM. He must have had a nightmare or something. Anyway, I started thinking about the woman in the shadows on the video recorded in the Port Authority Bus Terminal. Bingo! If she wasn't from Syracuse, then she must have come from Washington. And now that we had a picture of her, albeit an artificially aged composite, I thought, what the hell, why not run it through the FBI's Next Generation Identification system. The NGI database contains all sorts and manner of data, including mugshots, iris scans, DNA records, and the like. Some of the data were captured through a nationwide network of cameras and databases.

"I figured maybe your perp might have been charged with a crime at some point and her mugshot ended up in the database. Or maybe she applied for a passport or some other form of identification that required a picture and maybe even her fingerprints. I didn't know, but it was worth a shot.

"So, I stumbled in here around 6 this morning, put on a pot of coffee, and launched a search."

Martelli was impressed. "Wow, that was a brilliant idea. I'm serious. But there must be tens of millions of facial images in that database. I would have guessed you wouldn't get a hit in a month of Sundays."

"I was concerned about that as well. But the fact is, Lou, the system can match a single face from among 1.6 million mugshots or passport photos with 92 percent accuracy in less than 1.2 seconds. I mean, this thing is so fast it will blow your mind.

"I had the woman's identity nailed pretty quickly. But knowing you wouldn't be in yet, I used the time to do some research on her."

"Were you able to learn anything?" Martelli inquired.

"This is one interesting woman, Lou. It's like she appeared out of nowhere sometime around 2000. There is absolutely no sign of a person with the name Mackenzie Pierce having the background of this woman prior to that time, at least no one I can find.

"Her *curriculum vitae* contains references only to scientific papers published in the last five years. She has nothing listed prior to that. Yet there's no question the college degrees she earned, including a doctoral degree, are legit because I found her listed as an alumnus on her university's Website."

"Where was the university?"

"In a western state, as I recall. Let me look again. Here it is. Idaho."

"Good place to stash a family."

"Anything else of interest?" asked Sean.

"Oh, yes, and you'll really like this. If you go to the Internet Website WhitePages.com and search on Mackenzie Pierce in the greater Washington, DC, area, you find only one person by that name living in Alexandria, Virginia. She's listed at an address just south of Ronald Reagan Washington National

Airport. Listed under people Mackenzie Pierce knows is someone named Allison Pierce ... *age 19.*"

No one spoke for a moment. It was Sean who broke the silence. "She was pregnant when her family, then using the name Hughes, pulled up stakes and left Syracuse!"

Martelli shook his head. "Well I'll be damned. No wonder her father panicked and the family disappeared so quickly. If they were in the Witness Security Program, the last thing they and the authorities needed was the gossip and attention associated with their daughter's pregnancy. It was safer for the authorities to move the family to another part of the country, give everyone new identities, and start them over again. And given the circumstances, it had to be done quickly."

O'Keeffe concurred. "You got that right, Lou, and what do you want to bet Allison Pierce's father is none other than our second vic, Trent Morrison?"

"Don't be so sure," countered Martelli. "The King may have graced one of his favorite devotees, Brian Hallaway the Younger, with Tia Hughes' favors. So we still need to understand the exact role Hallaway played in this tragedy."

Martelli stood and started pacing behind his desk. He took two silver dollars from his pocket—the same coins his father had carried for years when he was on the Force—and started flipping them over and over again between his fingers like they were poker chips.

Holding the coins always brought him comfort. One was a worn 1882 'Morgan' minted in New Orleans. The other 'cartwheel,' a 1922 'Morgan,' had been minted in Philadelphia. Lou's dad, Pietro, a deceased New York street cop, had carried them in his pocket until the day he died in a hail of bullets from the guns of two escaped felons he had tracked to and mortally wounded in a warehouse on the docks in lower Manhattan.

Pietro was a religious man and a Good Samaritan as well. Some thought the two pieces of silver he carried harkened back to the story of the Jewish man who was traveling from Jerusalem to Jericho when he was attacked by bandits. Left for dead, the traveler was saved by a despised Samaritan, who paid an innkeeper two pieces of silver to take care of the traveler.

The story befitted the manner in which Pietro conducted his life. On the day he was buried, Martelli's mother, Rosalia, insisted Louis keep the coins as mementos and a reminder of how his father would have hoped he would carry on the Martelli name. The coins have been his constant companions ever since.

Martelli stopped pacing and looked at the picture of his father on the wall in his office. He appeared to be deep in thought. "Given everything we know now, Sean, one thing is abundantly clear. Chapman's life is in imminent danger!"

Thirty-six

Captain Frank Emerson had been a member of the Alexandria Police Department since 1991, rising from the rank of patrolman to being elected to the highest position on the Force in 2008. Well respected in the small independent city just to the south of the nation's capital, the area is home to some of the most important historic sites associated with the American Revolutionary War and the War Between the States. This morning, sitting in his office on Wheeler Avenue, the chief was rapidly taking notes as he listened to a detective-investigator of the New York Police Department. Martelli had just given Emerson everything he knew about Mackenzie Pierce. As well, he had simultaneously forward the picture of Pierce that Dugan had downloaded from the National Archives for Ancient Cultures Website.

"We need your help in finding Pierce, Captain Emerson. We have every reason to believe she's behind two murders, one in Syracuse a few years ago, and another more recently in Manhattan. Both were men she attended high school with in the mid-1990s who we believe were involved in her assault, rape, and pregnancy.

"We also have reason to believe she'll kill again. This time the target will be a third man from that school, someone we think was also involved in that rape."

"I understand completely, Lou. And please call me Frank. I'll send a black and white out to her residence and pick her up if possible. At the same time, we'll put out a local BOLO for her and her daughter. Do you want me to call the National Archives for Ancient Cultures or is that something you'd rather do."

"If you don't mind, I'd like to take first crack at it. I'm still a little unsure about how I'm going to approach those folks without them tipping her off."

"It's your call. But please, keep me in the loop. We'll do everything we can to support you on this."

"I absolutely will, Frank. And I sincerely appreciate your help."

"Not a problem. Oh, Lou, one last thing before we hang up. Have you thought about the possibility she may already be in New York?"

"That's what's keeping me up at night. I've alerted the 24th Precinct to keep an eye on Chapman's apartment building, which is on West 86th Street near Riverside Drive. My guess is, if she's in the city, she'll either approach the building from the 1 Line MTA subway stop on Broadway or by cab. Either way, it's going to be difficult. She strikes at night, has worn a veil to cover her face on one occasion, and uses her history with these men to gain their trust. Once she's with them, she plies them with liquor laced with chloral hydrate, and when their lights go out, she injects them with heroin. It's a quick

174

death, to be sure, and one easily attributable to suicide by drug overdose."

"Interesting way to settle old scores. But why kill them now, after all these years?"

"That's the $64,000 question, Frank, and one we certainly want to ask her, believe me."

"All right, we'll try to find her from this end. Let me know what you learn from talking with her employer."

"I'll get back to you as soon as I know something."

■ *Theodore Jerome Cohen*

Thirty-seven

'I will get the director for you, Detective." Martelli sat in his office listening to a performance of Max Bruch's Concerto for Violin, Opus 26 on his telephone headset. Evelyn Baylor, the executive assistant to the director of the National Archives for Ancient Cultures, had just put Martelli on hold while she went to look for her boss.

The National Archives for Ancient Cultures was housed in an imposing stone edifice in the heart of the District of Columbia. Like many buildings in the area, its back was to the Mall while the main entrance faced Constitution Avenue. The Archives were world renowned for its research as well as the quality of its collection of ancient artifacts, displays, and library. The Archives enrolled scholars from around the world in its advanced program of studies, including an extensive curriculum of courses on forensic anthropology, an area in which the Archives excelled. Its current director, Helen Watson, PhD, had been with the organization for more than 30 years. As the author of more than ten books in the fields of Greek and Roman cultures, she was one of the most respected anthropologists in the Western Hemisphere.

"Good morning, Detective Martelli? And how are you this fine morning?"

"I'm good, Dr. Watson. And you?"

"Well, Detective. To what do I owe this honor?"

"Well, we're trying to tie up some loose ends on a case up here involving something that happened a week ago in the Port Authority Bus Terminal on 8th Avenue."

She laughed. "And you're calling *me* about that?"

Martelli chuckled. "Yes, I know, it sounds strange. But a passenger on a Washington to New York bus lost her purse. She was insistent as to where she was sitting, even telling us her seatmate mentioned she worked in Washington on studies of ancient cultures. The woman insisted the seatmate didn't take the purse, but hoped she might have seen something or someone that would help her get it back. Apparently it contained some family heirlooms, so you can understand her anxiety and the urgency of the matter."

"I'm sorry, Detective, but I still don't see what this has to do with me or the Archives."

"I understand, Doctor. And I apologize. I should have been more direct.

"We showed the woman photographs on the Internet of people who work at various organizations around Washington that are associated with ancient cultures. It took quite some time, as you can imagine, given the presence of the Smithsonian and various universities and colleges. But finally, she identified Dr. Pierce of your staff as the person who was seated on the bus next to her.

"We've attempted to reach Dr. Pierce—I understand she lives in Alexandria—but have been unsuccessful. Nor, I'm told by your assistant, is she in this morning. So, I thought I'd touch base with you and see if you might know where she could be."

"Okay, now I understand, Detective Martelli. It all makes sense. I just looked up Dr. Pierce's current timecard, and indeed, she did take some vacation earlier this month. So, it's entirely possible she traveled to New York when you say. I know she loves the theater and often travels to your city with her daughter to see shows on Broadway. Sometimes she goes alone, leaving her daughter with friends or colleagues."

"Have you known her long?"

"Heavens, yes. I hired her. She came highly recommended by her former employer, the Department of Justice. Her background in forensic anthropology complemented well the experience and capabilities of our other staff members, and the courses she teaches always are filled to capacity. She also performed an extensive suite of research projects on Greek and Roman cultures, work for which she often was honored. In fact, she recently published a number of seminal papers on subjects of major interest to the scientific community in some very prestigious journals."

Martelli laughed. "What does she do in her spare time, assuming she has any?"

"Well, I didn't socialize much with her. But I understand she dotes on her daughter. Others on the staff tell me mother and daughter frequently take long bicycle rides from their home on the south side of the Alexandria down the bike path that

179

runs alongside the George Washington Parkway to Mount Vernon, stopping on occasion for a picnic on the banks of the Potomac River across from Fort Washington. And of course, with all the museums and parks in the greater Washington area, there is no end of things for them to enjoy here.

"In short, I suspect Dr. Pierce leads quite a balanced life, and one that certainly embraces her daughter's needs."

"Do you have any idea where she could be at this moment? I'd really like to talk with her. It's possible we could clear up this entire matter of the missing purse in one telephone call."

"Well, if she's not here, it's possible she could be at a doctor's appointment or with her daughter. There's nothing in her timecard to indicate she's taken vacation or sick leave. I can ask her colleagues if she mentioned taking some time off today and call you back if I learn anything, Detective. But that's the best I can do at this time."

"Well, you've been most helpful, Dr. Watson. I'm sure your assistant has my telephone number on her console. If you hear from Dr. Pierce, perhaps you'd be so kind as to have her call me. We really would like to help the woman she sat with recover her family heirlooms."

"I'll do what I can, Detective."

Thirty-eight

'F'rank, this is Lou Martelli. I just talked with Helen Watson, director of the National Archives for Ancient Cultures. Dr. Pierce is not at work today. My gut tells me she's on the move, perhaps already up here in New York."

"I was just about to call you, Lou. After we hung up earlier, I sent a black and white to Pierce's townhouse, as promised. No answer. The patrolman talked with a few neighbors. One said she saw Pierce get into a cab yesterday. Based on a description of the cab and the time the cabbie picked up Dr. Pierce, we were able to confirm it took her to National Airport. I'm afraid she may already be in New York."

"I figured as much. Based on our information, the man we believe she's going to kill next will arrive back in the States sometime later today. We'll make every effort to talk with him upon his arrival, but there's no assurance we'll be successful.

"Did you have any luck picking up Pierce's daughter?"

"No, she's probably with her friends, so there's no telling where she might be. All we can do is to continue to look for her."

"All right, stay in touch if you find her or hear anything. I'll do likewise. And Frank, we sincerely appreciate your help."

Martelli and O'Keeffe spent the remainder of the day working on paperwork associated with the Morrison and Hallaway homicides. According to the information they previously had received from Chapman's secretary, his flight wasn't expected to arrive at John F. Kennedy International Airport until a few minutes after 9 PM that evening. Two patrolmen were assigned to meet him at the luggage carousel and apprise him of the situation. Two other patrolmen soon would be stationed in front of Chapman's apartment building to arrest Pierce if she was spotted in the area.

"You hungry, Lou?"

Martelli looked at his watch. It was a little after 7 PM. "Yeah, I guess I am. Why, are you heading out to pick up some sandwiches?"

O'Keeffe nodded. "This could be a long night. If you want, I'll run over to that deli in the Fifth Precinct and spring for a couple of corned beef on rye with mustard, some cole slaw, and a few pickles. We can grab two Coke's out of the machine in the hall."

"Sounds good to me."

O'Keeffe took off, leaving Martelli to continue work on the Department's files.

More than ten minutes had passed when Martelli suddenly had a look of panic on his face. *We haven't checked in with*

Chapman's secretary for several days. What if his plans changed?

Martelli grabbed his cell phone, flipped through the various entries in his directory, and finding Chapman's office number, quickly initiated a call to his secretary.

"Dan Chapman's Office, Margaret speaking."

"Margaret, this is Detective Martelli. I'm so glad I caught you before you left for the day. I just want to make sure Mr. Chapman is still expected to arrive at John F. Kennedy International Airport around 9 PM tonight."

"Oh no, Detective. He caught a flight out of London very early this morning. As a matter of fact, he arrived home a few hours ago."

Beads of sweat appeared on Martelli's brow. "Thank you, Margaret. Have a good evening."

Martelli ran up the stairs and to his car, calling O'Keeffe on the way. "Sean, we have a problem. Chapman's already home. For all we know, he's in his apartment with that woman. Call for backup and meet me at Chapman's as soon as you can get there. I hope we're not too late."

No sooner had Martelli ended the call with his partner than he received a call from Central. "Detective Martelli, I'm going to patch a call through to you from Officer Murtaugh of the Central Park Precinct. Please stand by."

Martelli heard a click on the line. "Detective Martelli, this is Patrolman Murtaugh. I don't know if you remember me. I worked that case with you a few years ago when that guy was beheaded in Central Park."

"Yes, Murtaugh, I remember."

Juggling his phone, Martelli actuated his car's red, dash-mounted, rotating beacon, threw the car into Drive, and tore away from the curve, heading toward the Upper West Side.

"Well, Detective, I was just taking a break over on the West Side—you know, stopping in a bodega on Broadway to grab a bite—when I saw a woman step out of the 86th Street subway stop. I wouldn't have paid any attention to her except she was wearing a rather fashionable hat *with a black veil*. Who the hell wears veils these days on the street? Maybe in church, but on the street?

"And then I remembered reading a BOLO for the perp in that Morrison case. You described a video taken at the bus terminal that showed a person of interest wearing a veil. I just thought you should know."

"Did you happen to see which way the woman was headed?"

"Oh, yes . . . down toward West End Avenue, perhaps to Riverside Drive."
"Thanks, Murtaugh. I'll notify the black and whites assisting me. You'll never know how important your call is. Believe me, your supervisors will be made aware of your good work."

"Thank you, sir. I hope you catch the perp!"

Dammit, though Martelli. *She's going to kill him, if she hasn't already. And as usual, we're sitting here with our thumbs up our collective asses!*

He pushed the accelerator to the floor, waving his left hand back and forth, yelling and cursing as if the other drivers actually could hear him. A cab cut him off as he was about to change lanes, forcing him to stand on his breaks and lean on the horn. Even though the cabbie couldn't hear him, Martelli started yelling at the top of his lungs. "Get the fuck out of the way, you asshole. Official police business!"

The cabbie gave him the finger.

What's new? Martelli thought.

O'Keeffe was ten minutes behind Martelli. And he was facing similar if not worsening traffic problems.

At best, the traffic could be described as 'controlled mayhem.' Even with his rotating beacon and siren, it took Martelli almost 20 minutes to reach Chapman's apartment building. Pulling his car abruptly to the curb, he left the front-end blocking the sidewalk. Leaving the rotating beacon flashing on the dash and locking the car, he half-ran, half-skipped to Chapman's building. There, in front, was a black and white with two officers having coffee. They obviously were *not* paying attention to what was going on around the building. A few sharp comments from Martelli sent the coffee flying, with one officer posted to the front door and the other running for the service entrance in the rear.

Martelli entered the apartment building, displayed his badge to the doorman, and ran for the elevators. "Chapman's Apartment?"

"Top floor, 45C," the doorman shouted back.

The doors to one elevator were just opening and a couple stepped forward to enter. "Sorry, police business. This won't be making any stops."

Scowling, they stepped back as Martelli commandeered the lift. Once inside, and with the doors closed, Martelli pressed both the '45' and 'Close Door' buttons simultaneously, not releasing his fingers until the car started to move. This slight-of-hand trick ensured him of an uninterrupted run to the top floor.

Come on, come on . . . can't you go any faster?

Martelli watched the display above the doors click off the floors . . . *5, 6, 7 . . . 22, 23, 24 . . . Come on, come on, will you?* *. . . 43, 44, 45.*

The elevator stopped and the doors opened. Martelli was out in an instant, half-running, half-hopping toward Apartment 45C. As he drew his revolver, he caught sight of someone who appeared to be a woman running out of the apartment and toward the end of the hallway. Before he could call out, however, she, having spied him, disappeared through the fire door leading to the roof.

The door to the Chapman's apartment was open, and from the hall, Martelli could see the man on the floor. What appeared to be a syringe was sticking out of his left arm. A glass of Scotch or some other spirit was on the coffee table beside him.

Entering cautiously with gun drawn, Martelli kneeled and felt for a pulse. There was none.

Grabbing his phone, Martelli dialed Central and requested a 'bus' be sent to Chapman's apartment. Then, pushing himself up with the help of the coffee table, he turned and ran for the stairs leading to the roof.

It was a steep climb, but once at the top, he opened the roof shed's door, stepped over the threshold, and saw the lights of Union City, West New York, and West Bergen, NJ across the Hudson River. The full Moon was beginning its ascent. It was only when he took a few steps onto the roof and looked slightly to his right that he saw Mackenzie Pierce. She was standing on the low brick wall at the front of the building, preparing to jump.

Fortunately, Martelli, in 2012, had undergone intense training on how to handle situations such as this. He slowly approached the woman in a relaxed, non-threatening manner. "Dr. Pierce, I'm Detective Louis Martelli. Can we talk?"

Pierce seemed surprised Martelli had called her by name. But she recovered quickly, and though appearing intent on finishing what she had come to do, was curious as to how the detective had come to know her identity. "Are you sure who I am, Detective?"

"Perhaps I should address you as Celestia Hughes."

She laughed. "You're not even close. Why do I get the feeling our conversation is becoming something akin to the story of Rumpelstiltskin, who posed a riddle regarding his name to Graham, son of Sir Hereward?"

Martelli said nothing.

"I'm sorry Detective if levity ill-befits the moment. But you must understand, who I am is the farthest thing from my mind right now. I haven't had an identity to call my own since I was five years old. So, of what importance is it to you or anyone else who I'm known as today?"

"Just out of curiosity, Dr. Pierce or Ms. Hughes, or whoever you are, who were you when you were five years old?"

She looked at him and smiled. "There once was a little girl I knew named Amanda Cooper, who used to run and play with her friends in a place quite far from here. Then, one day, she and her parents were moved to a place in the northern part of New York and given new identities."

"Why was that? What happened to cause them to have to move?"

She shifted her body slightly, almost losing her balance. Martelli appeared to stop breathing.

"My father wouldn't talk about it. Some years later, however, when I was older, my mother told me it had something to do with the people my father worked for and the testimony he gave in court against them. Apparently, it put all of our lives in jeopardy."

"Was it difficult growing up and having to learn to be another person?"

"Not really. My mother and I made it into a game. After a while it was fun, like being in a play. Pretty soon, Amanda Cooper no longer existed. In her place was Celestia Hughes. I loved that name. It was something that belonged in the heavens, like the stars. All the boys called me Tia. I loved that nickname."

Dammit, thought Martelli, *where is Sean? I could use some help up here, Buddy. And forget about using a life net. It would be totally worthless from these heights!*

Pierce started to pace back and forth on the low brick wall, which being a foot-and-a-half wide, provided little if any leeway for missteps. But years of walking on narrow scaffolding at major archaeological digs in Europe and the Middle East rendered the scientist immune to the effects of heights.

Heights, on the other hand, made Martelli queasy—unless, of course, his feet were firmly planted on the metal floor of a US Army UH-60 Black Hawk or some commercial jet liner of American or European manufacture. The detective still took ribbings from his family about what happened on their late-summer trip one year to Cancun, Mexico, which featured a side trip to Chichen Itza. At the top of the Kukulkan Pyramid, Stephanie and the kids had no concerns whatsoever when it came to walking around the platform, venturing dangerously close to its edges at times. Martelli, on the other hand, though almost never at a lack for confidence, was content to take in the view from a point only inches from the wall of the pyramid's temple.

Pierce's eyes appeared to be focused on Riverside Drive below and on the thinning rush hour traffic.

Martelli edged closer.

"Don't think I can't see what you're doing, Detective."

Martelli froze.

"So, how did you lose your leg?" Pierce, if anything, was as perceptive as a hawk circling at 200 feet, looking for a mouse in the field below.

"Oh, that. I was a crewman on a Black Hawk during the April, 2003 invasion of Baghdad. We were one of six choppers flying toward the city when our aircraft experienced engine failure—something having to do with the oil filtration system, as I recall. Anyway, our pilot put down in a field, and a maintenance team flew in and fixed the problem. But by the time they made things right, it was dark. We tried to catch up with our tactical group, but ten miles south of Baghdad we took a hit and went down. The pilot and co-pilot never made it out. I got blown out of the cargo door when the fuel tanks exploded, but unfortunately, the blast destroyed my left leg.

"Some months later, an officer told me—and he said he'd deny ever talking with me if I repeated the story—friendly fire brought us down."

Philips shook her head. "Wow, isn't that always the case! The ones you think you can trust are the ones that bring you down . . . in your case, quite literally."

"Well, the same thing happened to you, didn't it?"

"What are you talking about?" she snapped.

"Just saying. I think everything was going well for you at the Marquis de La Fayette High School until someone betrayed your trust at the start of your junior year, and that was the end of Celestia Hughes."

"She froze and turned her gaze toward him. "What the hell do you know about that?"

Martelli was about to respond when his cell phone rang.

■ *Theodore Jerome Cohen*

Thirty-nine

Martelli looked at Pierce. She shrugged as if she could care less. Martelli knew from the ringtone it was O'Keeffe. "It's my partner. Do you mind if I take it?"

"Makes no difference to me."

Martelli pulled the phone from his pocket, and swiping the screen, opened the link. "Yes, Sean. I thought you'd be here by now."

"Well, the goddamn traffic coming uptown is unbelievable. There's been a five-alarm fire in the mid-60s—natural gas explosion, I think—and everything is gridlocked. So, with detours and all, it's going to be a while before I can get there. Are you all right?"

"Oh, yes, Dr. Pierce and I are just taking in the night air on the roof of Chapman's apartment building. We're doing fine."

"Okay, hold the fort. I'll be there as soon as I can."

Martelli ended the call and put the phone in his pocket. "Good man, O'Keeffe. Wish he were here with me now."

"He couldn't help you, Detective, believe me. So, you were saying."

"Well, I think I've been able to piece together most of your story, at least the part concerning what happened in high school. Still, there are a few things I haven't been able to figure out."

As a scientist, Pierce was intrigued. She stopped pacing and looked at Martelli. "Such as . . .?"

"How did you get mixed up with Morrison and Hallaway? We know you were dating Dan Chapman, so what happened?"

She laughed and shook her head. "I don't know why I'm laughing. Maybe it's my way of keeping it all together . . . you know, it's like after all these years, you still can't get rid of all the hurt and pain and anger. And at some point you only can take so much, shed so many tears, before the only way to preserve your sanity is to laugh." She ran her hands through her long blonde hair.

Obviously, Martelli had struck a raw nerve. He said nothing.

"Danny the Betrayer. Danny Boy. My steady . . . at least until that party one September night early in our junior year when Trent came up to him and asked Danny if he could take me out on a date. Danny was reluctant at first but Trent, being Trent, persisted. Within a week, Trent and I double-dated with Brian Hallaway and his date. Of course, by then I no longer was going steady with Danny.

194

"A week later, at another party, Trent got me drunk. He wanted to have sex, and I pushed him away, over and over again, but he forced himself on me. Then, Brian took his place. If it hadn't been for my friend Derek Hamilton, I never would have gotten home that night.

"A month later I learned I was pregnant. When my dad found out, he alerted the people in the Witness Security Program. My parents were furious, but there was nothing they could do. To file charges would have risked the possibility of compromising our identities. So, two days later, the government moved us to Idaho, and we started over again as the Pierces.

"Our religion prevented me from having an abortion, and I'm glad. I love my daughter and frankly, Detective, she is the one good thing that has come into my life."

"Where is she now?"

"Well, I hope she's with some college friends, perhaps hiking in the Blue Ridge Mountains of Virginia. I can't think of a better pastime. We always took long bicycle rides and hikes when time permitted. The greater Washington area is simply full of wonderful opportunities for outdoor activities."

Martelli nodded.

"So, killing Hallaway, Morrison, and now Chapman was, pure and simple, revenge for what they had done to you in high school?"

"Nothing more, nothing less. They destroyed the life I had built out of the ashes of my family's earlier life. So, I vowed to one day destroy theirs, *no matter how long I had to wait.* Not the most laudatory of life's goals, was it, Detective? Nevertheless, it was mine.

"But you said there were a *few* things you still hadn't figured out. What else has you puzzled?"

She turned and walked a few feet away from Martelli, all the while keeping an eye on him.

"Why wait until now . . . or rather, until two years ago, when you put Brian Hallaway in his grave. And why start with him? Why not go after Morrison first? He was the one who set everything in motion?"

She threw her head back and laughed. "Well, aren't you just full of questions this evening, Detective? But those are easily answered.

"First, you have to understand, my mother passed away of breast cancer in late 2006."

"I am sorry, Doctor. You have my condolences."

"Thank you. Mom suffered from breast cancer for many years. Her death was a blessing.

"Then my father passed a few years later. At that point, I opted out of the Witness Security Program and moved to Alexandria, Virginia with my daughter. The Department of Justice was very helpful in getting me the job with National

Archives for Ancient Cultures in Washington. And frankly, why shouldn't they have? My father helped them achieve more than 17 convictions in federal court and recover more than $5 billion for various victims. And other than my pregnancy, we never gave them one problem in all the years we were in the program.

"So, I was free to pursue my own agenda. I started looking at what had become of Morrison, Hallaway, and Chapman. With the Internet, it was easy to find information, and Hallaway, with all of his problems, was in the Syracuse newspaper constantly. He was an easy target. Here was a man already troubled with alcohol and drugs, in and out of treatment centers, and toward the end, living on the street. Killing him hardly presented a challenge.

"I made two trips to Syracuse. He almost recognized me on the first trip. I saw him start to cross the street and walk in my direction. Fortunately, I managed to duck into the shadows before he could get to me. On my second trip, I found him alone, very drunk, shooting up in an alley. I confronted him as a friend who wanted to put the past behind us."

"What did he say?"

"He was hesitant at first, but then warmed to the idea. I offered him a stiff drink, which he accepted, and when he fell over, I injected him with some of his own heroin. I didn't even need to use the chloral hydrate I had brought with me. He stopped breathing within two minutes. I took the rest of his heroin with me to use on Morrison and Chapman. Frankly, I was surprised at how easy it was to kill Hallaway."

"And Morrison."

"I simply called him from the bus terminal and talked about letting bygones be bygones. He asked about having dinner the next night, and I agreed. But I stood him up and waited outside the restaurant while he was inside, giving him an excuse for my being late when he finally emerged.

"As I assumed he would, he asked me to come to his townhouse for a nightcap and a chat . . . you know the story. He already had had a few drinks by the time he left the restaurant, so getting him to down one more, this one laced with chloral hydrate, was easy. In went the heroin, and that was that. He died within three minutes. I cleaned up the place to erase any sign I was there, rinsed his glass and poured him half a glass of fresh wine, took his house key, locked the door behind me, and left."

"What did you do with key if I may ask?"

Pierce laughed. "Well, I doubt you'll find it, Detective. I threw it in a sewer at Penn Station the next morning when I went to catch my train back to Washington. Have you ever ridden the Acela Express on the Northeast Corridor? It's really quite civilized you know."

Martelli chuckled. The irony of her last statement did not go unnoticed.

"And Chapman?"

"He was all too happy to put the past behind us and start over again. Overjoyed might be a better word, Detective. I think he still loved me and felt guilty over what had happened. When the doorman told him I was in the lobby, I could sense from what I heard on the loud speaker he could barely contain his enthusiasm over seeing me again. He had drinks already poured when I arrived. I don't think I was there three minutes before I spiked his Scotch. He was dead five minutes later.

Pierce looked at Martelli and feigned a frown. "Then you had to come along and spoil the reunion." She chuckled. "And to think I might have gotten away with it."

Martelli shook his head. It appeared he couldn't believe what he was hearing. Pierce was confessing to three murders with all the emotions of a woman discussing a shopping excursion with a friend.

"By the way, Detective, those cops you had stationed outside Chapman's building . . . they didn't give me a second glance. But then, I think the one in the passenger seat was staring at my cleavage. And yes, I wasn't wearing a veil."

"And the coins? What about them?"

Pierce smiled. "Pure whimsy. I had three of them, you know. I acquired them on a recent archaeological expedition in Europe. They seemed so apropos. I thought it would be simply terrible if they went to waste.

"Did you find them perplexing, Detective? I hope so. They were meant to be a bit of a tease. I'm sorry I wiped the fingerprints off them before carefully depositing them by their edges in the deceased's mouths, but I'm sure you understand."

Pierce started humming softly, nodding her head now and then as if she were carrying on some sort of conversation in her head. She was off in her own world.

Time's running out, thought Martelli. *I can't keep her talking much longer. Where the hell is O'Keeffe? I wonder if he picked up my hint about the roof . . . and if he did, whether or not he even did anything about it, given the fire downtown.*

"Why don't you come down and let me get you some help, Doctor Pierce?"

She appeared startled "Huh? Oh! It's too late for that, Detective. We both know that. I've lived in a prison all my life. With the exception of my earliest years, I've been forced to live a life of lies, using names and identities made up out of whole cloth. There never was a time I could say to anyone, 'This is who I am. This is my name. This is where I'm from. These are my parents, Joyce and Leonard Cooper. Let me tell you about our life together. It was really quite exciting.

"Frankly, Detective, it's time to put an end to the charades. It's time to end it all."

"What about your daughter."

Pierce did not say anything for a few seconds. She turned away, looking first across the river, then down at the street. Finally she turned toward Martelli. "She's strong. She'll understand once she knows the truth."

"But it doesn't have to end this way, Doctor, for her sake if no one else's."

"She knows I love her, Detective. Nothing could ever change that."

Watching her, Martelli saw what he perceived as a slight flexing in her knees.

It's now or never, he thought. Ever so slowly, he inched toward her.

Then, he sprang, throwing his arms around her waist. She slipped through his grasp and fell over the side, dragging Martelli with her over the ledge.

Instinctively Martelli clenched his knees together, hugging the ledge while at the same time grabbing Pierce's left arm with his right hand.

Sweat poured from his brow as he tried to prevent the woman from falling. But it was futile. His hand was wet with sweat, and she was slipping from his grasp. Ever so slowly he and Pierce were being pulled to their deaths by the inexorable force due to gravity.

Oh God, prayed Martelli, *please don't let it end this way.*

■ *Theodore Jerome Cohen*

<u>Forty</u>

Martelli's thighs were just about to lose their grip of the ledge when he felt a pair of strong hands—*O'Keeffe's hands*—grab his belt and stop him from falling. With his lower body now anchored firmly by O'Keeffe's weight, Martelli struggled to get a better grasp of Pierce's arm with both hands.

But the woman fought him at every turn, twisting and violently jerking her body to be free.

Finally, in one last desperate move, she kicked her body away from the side of the building, tearing loose from Martelli's grasp and falling away to her death on the sidewalk below.

Martelli could not take his eyes off hers as she fell toward the ground. They were wide open, staring blankly back at him. She never uttered a word as she disappeared into the shadow of the building and died instantly on the sidewalk below.

Struggling, O'Keefe pulled Martelli onto the roof, feet first, and they sat, out of breath, not saying anything for several minutes. The sound of fire engines could be heard approaching Chapman's building.

Finally, O'Keeffe spoke.

"You did everything you could, Lou. I don't know anyone who could have done more. It just wasn't to be."

Martelli, still shaken, nodded. "I don't know. What a tragedy. Here you have the rape of this beautiful young woman, and look how it changed the lives of so many people for the worse. Now, she and the three men who perpetrated the crime are dead, leaving only her child as an innocent victim. It all seems so unfair."

O'Keeffe stood and offered a helping hand to his partner. "Who told you life was fair, Lou?"

Epilogue

Mackenzie Pierce, PhD, aka Celestia (Tia) Hughes, whose birth name was Amanda Cooper, died instantly of blunt force trauma caused by a fall from the roof of a high-rise apartment building overlooking Riverside Drive on the Upper West Side of Manhattan. She was buried in Metairie, LA, in the Cooper family plot that is located in the cemetery next to the Metairie All-Saints Catholic Church. Her grave site is just to the right of her mother Joyce's. The funeral was private, with only her daughter and a few of her daughter's closest friends in attendance.

Deputy Coroner Michael Antonetti determined the deaths of Trent Morrison, Brian Hallaway, and Dan Chapman were the result of heroin overdoses exacerbated by excessive alcohol consumption. The cases were confirmed as homicides, with Mackenzie Pierce, PhD, cited as the killer in each instance.

Paternity tests performed using DNA from Allison Pierce, Trent Morrison, and Brian Hallaway showed Trent Morrison to be the father of Mackenzie Pierce's daughter. This being the case, Allison Pierce, through her lawyers, petitioned the court for her father's estate. She was subsequently awarded not only his Tribeca townhouse, Lamborghini *Huracán*, and other tangible possessions, but also, his stocks and commodity futures portfolios valued at more than $24 million.

Dillon Fitzpatrick, MD, medical examiner for the Onondaga County Health Department, received a Special Commendation from NYPD Police Commissioner Eugene Fields at a ceremony held in Fitzpatrick's honor at the Onondaga County Court House. The commendation and publicity attendant to the ceremony, which highlighted the part the medical examiner played in helping the City of New York solve Hallaway's murder, made him a shoo-in for re-reappointment in 2014.

The boyfriend of six-year-old Brianna Enriquez's mother was convicted on 13 counts of felony child molestation and sentenced to 52 years behind bars. He was still facing seven charges for assault, sexual battery, and rape brought against him by Brianna's mother when he was found dead in the prison exercise yard late one afternoon with a prisoner-made knife in his chest.

Detective-Investigator Louis Martelli and Detective-Specialist Sean O'Keeffe were lauded in a special, televised press conference held by New York Police Commissioner Fields. Seeing this, Principal IT Specialist Missy Dugan immediately forced both men to take her to dinner *and dancing* at the most expensive restaurant in Manhattan.

Theodore J. Cohen, PhD, holds three degrees in the physical sciences from the University of Wisconsin–Madison and has been an engineer and scientist for more than forty-five years. He has been an investor for more than fifty years and most recently, has focused on investigating and reporting on corruption in US financial institutions and agencies of the US government. His last novel was *Lilith: Demon of the Night*. Prior to this he wrote *House of Cards: Dead Men Tell No Tales*, a novel based on real events related to the 2008 financial crisis precipitated by the housing bubble. An earlier novel of the same genre, *Death by Wall Street: Rampage of the Bulls,* focused on corruption within the Food and Drug Administration (FDA) and the incompetence of the Securities and Exchange Commission (SEC). From December 1961 through early March 1962, Dr. Cohen participated in the 16th Chilean Expedition to the Antarctic. The US Board of Geographic Names in October, 1964, named the geographical feature Cohen Islands, located at 63° 18' S. latitude, 57° 53' W. longitude in the Cape Legoupil area, Antarctica, in his honor. Dr. Cohen's Antarctic Murders Trilogy describes what happened following a robbery of the Banco Central de Chile in Talcahuano in May, 1960. The robbery and the events that took place primarily between May 1960 and March 1962, are described in *Frozen in Time: Murder at the Bottom of the World* (Book I). *Unfinished Business: Pursuit of an Antarctic Killer* (Book II) reveals the events that unfolded between March 1962 and March 1965. *End Game: Irrational Acts, Tragic Consequences* (Book III) takes place in 1965 and resolves most, but not all, of the issues raised in the series. The Trilogy now is available as one (Kindle) edition, *Cold Blood*. Dr. Cohen's first novel, *Full Circle: A Dream Denied, A Vision Fulfilled*, which is based on his life as a violinist, was published in 2009. Dr. Cohen is a violinist in the Bryn Athyn (PA) Orchestra and particularly enjoys the music of Gustav Mahler. Finally, Dr. Cohen has published more than 400 papers, articles, columns, essays, and interviews, and is a co-author of *The* NEW *Shortwave Propagation Handbook* (from CQ Communications). For more information on Dr. Cohen and his novels, the interested reader is invited to view the book descriptions, photographs, and videos that can be found at <www.theodore-cohen-novels.com>.

Other Novels by Theodore Jerome Cohen

Death by Wall Street:
Rampage of the Bulls
Praise for *Death by Wall Street*

"From the first chilling moments, *Death by Wall Street* takes the reader inside the seamy nexus of Wall Street and Washington. Theodore Cohen has written the sad and tragic tale of how US financial markets and the pharmaceutical industry have 'captured' their regulators at the SEC and the FDA. Citizens beware!! Is this fiction? Sadly, it doesn't feel like it."
Mike Krauss, author of the forthcoming novel *Pursuits of Happiness,* is a columnist and commentator with a long career in US government and politics, and international business.

"*Death by Wall Street* may be a novel, but beneath its surface lies a terrible truth: the US financial markets, together with a sleeping US government, have caused the deaths of hundreds of thousands of citizens by denying them life-saving treatments."
Kerry M. Donahue, Esq., Chief Counsel, *Care To Live*

"*Death by Wall Street* is a 'must read' for anyone who has ever wondered why investing in biotech stocks is not for the faint-hearted. What Cohen reveals about stock manipulation, the SEC, and the FDA, will shock you."
Ed Silverman, Editor and Publisher, *Pharmalot.com*

House of Cards:
Dead Men Tell No Tales

Praise for *House of Cards*

"Gore Vidal once observed that historians are now writing fiction and novelists are writing history. In *House of Cards: Dead Men Tell No Tales,* Theodore Jerome Cohen has written the story of the monumental greed and fraud of the banksters who have subverted the American democracy. Maybe someday, the historians will catch up to him."
Mike Krauss is a director of the Public Banking Institute and is the author of the forthcoming novel *Pursuits of Happiness*

"Cohen brings Detective Louis Martelli to a new level of shady integrity, having him become a self-appointed judge and jury of right and wrong, good and bad."
Gary Sorkin for *Pacific Book Review*

"If you enjoy the 'ripped-from-the-headline' stories of shows like *Law & Order*, then you should definitely take a ride with [Cohen's] Lou Martelli and Missy Dugan."
Marty Shaw for *Reader Views*

"A real page turner! Beware. The next terrorist attack may be on our financial systems, *if it hasn't happened already!"*
Kerry M. Donahue, Esq., Attorney at Law

For more information, visit:
www.theodore-cohen-novels.com
or your preferred on-line retailer

Lilith:
Demon of the Night
Praise for *Lilith*

"Fast paced with snappy dialogue, likeable characters, and a touch of Middle Eastern mythology, this is a book that I could really sink my teeth into."
Paige Lovitt for *Reader Views*

"With more twists and turns than a Boa constrictor, the venomous plot unfolds and transports the reader from a modern-day, high-tech crime fighting novel into the dark side of cult practices within the mind of a serial murderer fixated on revenge. *Lilith* is a trophy on any shelf."
Gary Sorkin for *Pacific Book Review*

"Given the real-life vampire cases cited in the novel, one has to wonder if this isn't another of Cohen's 'ripped-from-the-headline' stories. Why aren't Hollywood producers calling about this gem?"
Irene Watson, Author of *The Sitting Swing* and *Rewriting Life Scripts*

"I've had a fascination with vampires ever since Italian researchers believe they found the remains of a female vampire from 16th-century Venice, buried with a brick in her mouth to prevent her feasting on plague victims. This macabre thriller will keep you on the edge of your chair to the very end."
Susan Violante, Author of *Innocent War: Behind An Immigrant's Past*
italianaustinite.com, blogtalkradio.com/vioradio

For more information, visit:
www.theodore-cohen-novels.com
or your preferred on-line retailer

Frozen in Time:
Murder at the Bottom of the World
Book I in the Antarctic Murders Trilogy
Praise for *Frozen in Time*

"A nasty little piece of skullduggery made all the more so by the fact this fictional tale is based on real events in the author's life."
Kirkus Discoveries

"Meticulously written, footnoted, including photographs, maps, memorabilia from the voyage, *Frozen in Time: Murder at the Bottom of the World* is an author's doctorate work in novel creation, hardbound with chilling cover art."
Gary Sorkin for *Pacific Book Review*

"*Frozen in Time* is compelling reading, combining the elements of conflict, suspense, intrigue, entertainment, and enlightenment. Highly recommended."
Richard R. Blake for *Reader Views*

"A fast read, with plenty of Chilean naval history and drama on the high seas in one action-packed novel full of big surprises."
Gary P. Priolo for *NavSource Naval History*

"[M]urder and mayhem blended with a dash of chilling drama!"
Deb Fowler for *Feathered Quill Book Reviews*

Frozen in Time: Murder at the Bottom of the World
Is *Recommended Reading* by Longitude®
(www.longitudebooks.com)

For more information, visit:
www.theodore-cohen-novels.com
or your preferred on-line retailer

Unfinished Business:
Pursuit of an Antarctic Killer
Book II in the Antarctic Murders Trilogy

Praise for *Unfinished Business*

"Theodore Jerome Cohen . . . is a master at creating an aura of mystery, suspense, and drama. Cohen's writing style is engaging, innovative, and focused, clearly designed for the post-modern reader."
Richard R. Blake for *Reader Views*

"It was Christmas in August as the FedEx package arrived with the 2nd of the Antarctic Murders Trilogy... [A] most enjoyable way to experience the Antarctic without having to put on a down parka."
Gary Sorkin of *Pacific Book Review*

"If you love reading a good psychological thriller and think you can stay one step ahead of a cunning murderer, you just might want to take a look at [*Unfinished Business* and] the Antarctic Murders Trilogy, a trilogy that will bring out the CSI in you!"
Deb Fowler for *Feathered Quill Book Reviews*

"Where Cohen fully succeeds is in drawing the complexity of Muñoz' character. ... With Muñoz so fully drawn, it will be a pleasure to learn his fate."
Kirkus Discoveries

Unfinished Business: Pursuit of an Antarctic Killer
Is *Recommended Reading* by Longitude®
(www.longitudebooks.com)

For more information, visit:
www.theodore-cohen-novels.com
or your preferred on-line retailer

End Game:
Irrational Acts, Tragic Consequences
Book III in the Antarctic Murders Trilogy
Praise for *End Game*

"As 'Birds of a feather flock together,' [the Antarctic Murder Trilogy] by Theodore Jerome Cohen should be packaged in a jacket and sold as a set because I certainly believe anyone hooked by the first chapter in the first novel will not be able to put this series down until all three books are finished.
Gary Sorkin for *Pacific Book Review*

"Cutting-edge drama and suspense, revealing characters through convincing dialog, provides the Antarctic Murders Trilogy with all the elements of a cutting-edge, award-winning, best-selling novel."
Richard Blake for *Reader Views*

"*End Game* will take you from the depths of an Antarctic crevasse to the top of the steeple of the Church of Saint Francis—La Iglesia de San Francisco—in search of the evil secrets of Captain Roberto Muñoz ... a man who cut his teeth at the feet of the insidious Larenas cartel!"
Deb Fowler for *Feathered Quill Book Reviews*

Jack Eadon Award for the Best Book in Contemporary Drama
Reader Views, 2011

End Game:
Irrational Acts, Tragic Consequences
Is *Recommended Reading* by Longitude®
(www.longitudebooks.com)

For more information, visit:
www.theodore-cohen-novels.com
or your preferred on-line retailer

The entire
**Antarctic Murders
Trilogy**
is available in
a <u>single</u>
Kindle edition
from
Amazon.com
as

Cold Blood

Full Circle:
A Dream Denied, A Vision Fulfilled
Praise for *Full Circle*

"Age is no barrier to setting goals."
Elizabeth Fisher, *Bucks County Courier Times*

"I wished wholeheartedly that it had been an autobiography! ... It is a very enjoyable read."
Elaine Richards, G4LFM, Radio Society of Great Britain (RSGB)

"*Full Circle* is an informative and accessible story that will be particularly enjoyed by musicians, electronic buffs and those who delight in family stories."
Joy Ward, *The Langhorne Ledger*

"I particularly enjoyed *Full Circle* because I identify to such a great extent with the author . . . [in music and career.]"
Edward Belanger, *Dials and Channels*, Journal of the Radio and Television Museum

"*Full Circle* is an inspirational read anyone, including young adults interested in amateur radio and/or music, will enjoy."
Dave Ingram, K4TWJ (SK), World of Ideas, *CQ* Magazine

For more information, visit:
www.theodore-cohen-novels.com
or your preferred on-line retailer

www.ingramcontent.com/pod-product-compliance
Lightning Source LLC
Chambersburg PA
CBHW061137170626
46809CB00003B/885